W9-CMZ-891

Break
 Every
Rule

Also by Carole Maso

Ghost Dance

The Art Lover

The American Woman in the Chinese Hat

AVA

Aureole

Defiance

For Anne,

Break
Every
Rule

Essays on
Language, Longing,
& Moments of Desire

Yours in the good fight,

Carole Maso

Carole Maso

COUNTERPOINT

WASHINGTON, D.C.

LIBRARY OF CONGRESS CATALOG CARD NUMBER: 00-022649
ISBN 1-58243-063-2

First Printing

Jacket and text design by Amy Evans McClure

Printed in the United States of American on acid-free paper that
meets the American National Standards Institute z39–48
Standard.

Counterpoint
P.O. Box 65793
Washington, D.C. 20035–5793

Counterpoint is a member of the Perseus Books Group

10 9 8 7 6 5 4 3 2 1

IN MEMORY—

John Hawkes

Zenka Bartek

Nathalie Saurraute

James Laughlin

Kathy Acker

William Burroughs

Marguerite Duras

William Gaddis

Allen Ginsberg

Robert Bresson

Contents

Break
 Every
Rule

The Shelter of the Alphabet

NEWPORT, RHODE ISLAND

*T*HIS IS THE PLACE I WILL BE CONCEIVED. In joy and love, with awe and fear—some fear. This is the place I will be made—next to water. And the longing for water shall never leave me. What are my parents, two kids from Paterson, New Jersey, doing here? That's my father, over there, stepping off a navy destroyer. It's 1955 and he's stationed here, and my mother has come to be near him. They love the song the water sings and the sailing songs. Later my mother will tell me that they read books aloud to one another and I like to imagine they read Yeats, and Melville, and maybe *Sonnets to the Portuguese* and other such conception texts. I like to imagine that language conjured me and the sea and these two people crazy for each other. Photos from this time reveal them to be so young: my mother golden blonde, with eyes the color of the sea. She is sitting next to a window, looking out—the window like the eye, transparent, suggestive, dazzling. And my father, a stringbean, a stick figure, though an ecstatic one, in a white sailor's suit. The pants with nobody in them, as we children will call him later.

I cannot from this distance hear their sighs or prayers, but I can imagine them. They are desirous, delirious, blindingly in love. But looking at these photos now, more closely, I see that something belies the surface joy. Of course. They have already had two miscarriages. I am wanted almost too much. Their devotion to the unknown future, their longing, is nearly palpable. After their lovemaking, in those first moments after my conception, there is absolute stillness, and prayers to the Virgin; they are wishing I might stick; they are hoping I might cling like a barnacle. My mother lies by the oceanside, lulled in blue, unmoving, my father's dreaming head resting on her breast— my small fin forming. Ocean child. Fin, small flipper. My mother says her rosary to the mysterious, silent Mary who smiles her wan smile. Great sorrow and great joy already live in me: sandwiched as I will be, on one side by two silky siblings who could not hold, and on the other side by a brother with a hole in his heart. But I am all health, I am all hope: I am miraculous, I am beloved from the start—and they make hope my home, my domain. I am desire and ocean, song and songs the blood sings. And they call me Carole, of course: song of joy. I am feared for and wanted beyond all reason. I live in their watery blue world of worry and desire, with the ghost images of the bodies that did not take.

Home is my mother's breath and blood. Home is my mother's voluptuous body and the darkness—the miracle of it and the ocean that cradled us. And their hope.

There must have been an element of ferocity…

There must have been an element of ferocity to have produced such a fierce child. To have made me at once so fierce and so mild.

Paterson is one of the great American poems, and it is a place, and it is the place where I was born and lived for a time. From the beginning home to me is a poem. I am born in a modernist masterpiece by William Carlos Williams. And in fact as I am being born he is completing Book Five of that opus, the book of the triumph of the imagination. Mysteriously he is handing this to me as I now begin to breathe. I am not surprised; it seems like destiny to me. And in the times of my illness, I will in fact believe I am the chosen one, handed this directly from him who wrote not for love or fame or because he wanted to say something, but to keep his sanity.

"It's a strange courage you give me, ancient star."

And yes, I am a daughter of Williams, who combined poetry, fiction, fact, criticism, bits of this and that in his work. A strange brew. I am his daughter as you, even if you know nothing of my work except this essay, will see. He has sent me on this charmed path.

"Rigor of beauty is the quest."

And then there is Allen Ginsberg, the other native of Paterson I grew up with. I adored his great heart and hunger, his music and outrage and audacity. His fallibility. How, as a teenager, I howled his Howl.

I feel thankful to have had these two as my literary fathers. It feels like a much more fortunate literary inheritance than my southern friends who have Faulkner to contend with. Williams, that troubled iconoclast, seems to me a far more benevolent, happy influence simply in terms of what he allows. Somehow Faulkner continues to look best far from home on the Latin American writers. I, as a North American, am grateful not to have to wear his necklace of crows and thorns.

Home is my father playing the trumpet—the music drifting. In Paterson. My grandfather's house has a stained-glass
window, and when my grandmother weeps, sick of this life,
sick of the burden of simply being herself, there is the stained
glass to focus on. My Grandpa Frank on the other side of town
—with his Armenia and his wife, who will not live long—
worked in the silk mills. Later, he will be beaten nearly to death
with the pipe he began to keep under his bed for protection.
Paterson, by then, having turned against us.

But not against me, not then.

Cadence was the block I lived on. Language my home.
Charmed one, I was born into a poem.

ERSKINE LAKE

Home was a blue lake in summer then and a man in a boat
who followed us as we swam its length and a woman who
taught us all the names of the wild flowers, and they were our
parents. I don't know how it happened and so quickly, but
suddenly there are five of us children. There is not one quiet
place. And I learn to build a place of silence and serenity and
space in some newly discovered zone of my brain. A place
where I might not only live, but flourish. Without it, there is
no interior life; without, it I sense I am going to die. Imagination was my home, my salvation then. The blue lake. The
space in me.

And my mother, too, is a consolation through the chaos,
constructing a safe universe, a world of love and stability in
which to experiment, play; a place of confidence where in those
long summers before school started she handed me the secret
key. As we sat next to the water, she taught me that glittering,
miraculous handful of charms—the alphabet. The child draws

the letter A and makes a home under its roof. She learns of the shade a T might cast. The light coming off K. The shelter of the letter M.

And my mother reads to me. All kinds of wondrous things: Wordsworth and Blake and Jarrell and Poe as I fall into a dream next to the lake's pale oval. A B C D...

VASSAR COLLEGE

Here I meet my triumvirate of women, the women who will be always true, always rigorous, demanding, loving, always urging me to the next place, always meeting me at least part of the way.

Helen. During our courtship in that Hudson Valley we pick apples. I recite Frost's "After Apple Picking" to her so that words and the apples become interchangeable—round, heavy, luscious, carrying sensual meaning: the apples, the language, and my strange love for this woman I have only just met. Everything becomes entangled; the apples falling, and the falling in love, and the delicious surrender to it all. Everything round and gorgeous and falling: home.

We in the nearly twenty years since that day have created a place—a familiar place, on which for the most part we can agree: home. A continuity. A kind of home is in her arms, in her enormous intelligence, in her flexibility, in her passion— and we are, despite everything, despite danger and madness and sorrow and addiction, safe. A little safe.

How did she know so long ago what it was I would need? We would need? How has she done it—continually been willing to reinvent, the world and our lives, so that we might not only continue, but thrive?

And at Vassar there is Miss Page, my beloved teacher, my

most trusted ally, my support, my role model. Everything about her awed and terrified me—a brilliance, an intelligence as I have never seen, a sensitivity, a discretion, an extraordinary intuition. And six-feet tall! She was everything. Miss Page, who allowed me my first chance to write, to try, even though I had been rejected from the creative writing senior central course where one wrote a creative thesis. And for many years I will be rejected over and over from almost everything—but not by Barbara Page and not by Helen. And not by my mother. What can they see that I can't? That no one else can?

Miss Page introduces me to the third woman—Virginia Woolf. We read her together in class. I begin to write. For the first time. And I am left permanently changed.

On almost any page of those luminous, beautiful novels I can find peace, challenge, the shock of recognition, company. One could live here, in lines like this, happily, for a long time. And I have done just that. In *To the Lighthouse, Mrs. Dalloway, Between the Acts, The Waves.*

And in fact I feel more at home there than just about any-where. And it is for the most part home enough to dispel the terrible house that mental illness builds, for the first time really during the time I am at Vassar—a place that will become so demanding and after a time so familiar that I do not have a choice but to live there. And chanting sentences is the only way to feel better finally. And writing sentences, making shapes, is the only way to feel better. Sustaining, miraculous language, that all these years keeps illness at bay. Dear Virginia Woolf. Dear Barbara, dear Helen. Dear fifty pages toward a novel I write as a senior in order to graduate. Maybe I will be saved.

Where we ran the ten blocks breathlessly because back then you got the *Village Voice* classifieds the night before and ran to each possibility and hoped somehow amid the crowds of people all wanting the same thing, you would somehow luck out and find a home in it all.

We did find one. We have kept it now since 1978. We will never give up these two rooms, and when I think of home as a place, this is the place I think of. Two minuscule rooms I share with you and our two cats on the edge of Soho in the West Village of Manhattan. I love you, though it doesn't always seem so obvious, and I love unreasonably these two altogether unremarkable little rooms. The place I have witnessed in every kind of light, at every time of day, and in every season. A place of so many intimacies, and revelations, and heartbreaks. Sometimes for breaks from writing I will talk to Mr. Angelo, our ancient, Greek superintendent, in the street; or bring my clothes to the Rastafarian tailor; or pray for whatever seems dire and impossible at Our Lady of Pompeii. In fact, we have grown up here together. The Minetta Tavern, the Van Dam Theater, the Bleecker Street Cinema, all the things that were once ours—now gone. I feel the accumulated memories of being long in a place—or at least having that place as a base. Here we bought the Christmas tree that year, here I kissed another, here is where we sweated under lights, dancing. Here, the corner where we wept, and here—all this—a place so resonant. If memories take up space and possess color, these streets are black by now from the overlapping of so many accumulated events. Here I lay down in the snow for hours, unable to imagine a way to go on.

How many times did we walk those same streets "dead drunk," and for once a phrase seems to fit, seems to make some sort of sense, "dead drunk," limping toward home? In all the sorrow and regret and frustration we could not express any other way back then.

But somehow we have survived. Survived the deaths and acquisition of cats, the thousand disappointments, all the drunkenness, all that we did to each other that was unforgivable and that we have somehow forgiven. All the good and bad news—and the devastating news—deaths of friends. This is where the calls come. This is where life seems unlivable and I get under the covers for days and days.

And you launch me again, sending me off on the next necessary thing I must do in order to write, to keep writing. You set me off for the first time in what will be many times, to do what I must do—and it doesn't finally somehow destroy us (though it sometimes comes close), but strengthens us in our love for each other and allows us to go on and change and grow and grow up. Much of the time we live off your student loans or a credit card or a meager salary or nothing. I go to my first artists' colony. It is the first time I am given months of uninterrupted time. When Yaddo says no, when MacDowell says no, when there is nothing, nowhere to go, there is Cummington, a community of the arts where artists are not guests but residents, a place that offers space and solitude in an excessively beautiful countryside. I stay for months and months on end.

NEW YORK CITY

And then I am back and suddenly Gary is dying. The new virus. Thus begins our long season of suffering. Of renunciation. Of fear. Of sorrow. Of good-bye.

And my first book is finally published. Without compromise. And with that, I am satisfied.

And then the phone call in the middle of the night: the first of October 1986.

PROVINCETOWN, MASSACHUSETTS

I am returned to the ocean, pale zygote, after a long separation. Back in silence to my one dreamy cell of being. Another new home. Provincetown in winter. The off-season. I am given a small studio at the Fine Arts Work Center. I have brought my few familiar things, my portable Virgin Mary, my pocket Sappho. I paint everything white. In this home at the end of the world—surrounded by water, desolate, beautiful—I enter my long period of mourning. Home of grief and water. Home of sorrow. Having for months counted T-cells, having learned the incredible shadow a T is capable of casting, I try to heal. I walk the streets, the dunes, the beaches. I go to the bars and St. Mary's of the Harbor.

If home is physical sanctuary, comfort, recognition, bliss, then home for me is Provincetown. Much of my earthly longing goes there. I ache for the place. It's a primal longing, a sexual one. It is the place I am most drawn to in the world. And irresistibly, and a little against my will, I keep returning there. I am a Pisces after all.

It's strange. I have lived now almost ten years without fear. Fear was a home and then it was not. Sadness was a home and then it was not anymore. And what could be worse? AIDS. I think of the urgency in me that Gary's death created. A monstrous acceleration, a new conviction to living, working— loving with a new recklessness, abandon, urgent, urgent. Gary who taught me to do everything, to be everything, to want, to have, to try everything—to not be afraid anymore.

VENCE, FRANCE

To keep living. To keep writing, to not tire. I get an NEA and decide to leave the country and live cheaply for a long time on the money. I choose an artists' colony in France called the Michael Karolyi Foundation.

It is perhaps the oddest and most strangely lovely time in my life. I am at once utterly at home and completely estranged and alone.

> What do I remember
> that was shaped
> as this thing is shaped?
> — *William Carlos Williams*

Stepping off the plane I am shocked to find that I remember this place, though I have never been here before. I remember clearly being a child, walking through a forest of small oaks, carrying a metal box of cinders to keep warm, with a woman who is my mother. She is not my Paterson mother, but another mother. I remember the war. There are terrible things, there are wondrous things outside the reach of my recollection, my consciousness, that are suddenly set into motion here. I, as a result, acquire a false sense of security, of belonging, of fluency. I am born for a second time into a different and distant home —a home from long ago. And I am filled with longing and unfinished things, and I feel unspeakable pain and sorrow at this intimation of a home which perhaps never existed and which I have been separated from, severed from until now. What else eludes me, I wonder, slips away? What else goes unremembered? I am bereft. A home I have been separated from and have forgotten and yet has haunted me. I have written about it from the start…France.

I think of all the things that are outside the range of our memories or imaginations or intelligence or talent—it's the place I suspect which is our true home. If we could get there we would finally feel okay. But we can't. We are all homeless, groping, roaming in the darkness, aware of only a fraction of it.

But I am delighted and in great awe over the resonances I can perceive. And the repetitions. At the Karolyi Foundation in the form of two extraordinary women, Judith Karolyi and Zenka Bartek, the reiteration again comes of who I am and why I live. I am reminded again of what I must do. It comes through with great force and clarity. They press me on, they press me further. I have stepped off the plane and into the care of these two women, lovers, both in their seventies, who offer me, like guardians at the doors of the psyche, fearlessness, diabolic and sometimes harsh judgments, support, and after awhile unconditional love. And they watch me unravel, as I will in the next months, and they will stand by and they will watch out for me, protect me, wait for me—as I too wait. Until I can take the vow again—having gone a long way off.

And in the New York I inhabited and left in 1988, my publishing house closes, and Helen, tired of all the separations, tired of all my antics, goes off with another woman, and I become lost. Almost irretrievably. I had left her again. Because I had to. But she was tired, bitter, lonely. Fed up finally.

I had left her behind, again—because I could not write—write, that is, on my own terms, without concern for the marketplace, without selling out in small but grave ways: writing for magazines, or teaching prematurely, or making unconscious decisions that might make the work more sexy, more accessible—but for all the wrong reasons. It seemed crucial not to derail myself now, not to subvert myself, not to give in. But she is less and less capable of understanding all this, or caring.

I was too afraid of not allowing my talent, my potential, to go where it needed to go.

I begin, as I often have, a long series of affairs. Because the body all along has been a kind of home to me. But I am sad, and deranged, and so far away. And I miss New York, and I miss her, but there's no place for me there, and no way I can afford to continue writing.

And I write down what happens because it is the only way I know to do. I write it all down, and eventually even it takes on the glow of the imagination, freeing itself from the known world. And I give it in the end a title of dislocation, my novel of France. I call it *The American Woman in the Chinese Hat.* I return to New York; I return to France. At some point Helen and I are reunited. I go back to France a third time. I am writing a wild, visionary thing, *The Bay of Angels*—but my precious time doesn't last, can't last.

AMERICA 1995

This country is not a home to me. I am tired of the America that has increasingly come to mean selfishness and avarice and cruelty and meanness of spirit. I have had it for good this time with the Republicans. I am disgusted by an America that loathes difference, otherness. An America indifferent to beauty. A country hostile to art and to its artists—and to all that makes life worth living in the first place. Ruskin wrote, "Great nations write their deeds in art." We are lost, violently

blinded, bankrupt. The children are hungry, the elderly are
frightened, the mentally ill wander the streets. Whose family
values are these? If it were not for the handful of people I love
too much, I would have found a way out of here by now.

I am leaving out many of my moves at this stage, many
changes of address; I tire. Other temporary residencies: Park
Slope; Washington, D.C.; Normal, Illinois. In four years, I
will teach in four schools; I despair. I am tired of roaming,
exhausted, depleted. About to give up.

HOUSE

It is a quiet September evening when the phone rings, and as
in a movie or a dream, the world changes in an instant. Various
people on the unreal speaker-phone saying "fiction," "prize,"
"fellowship." It's the Lannan Foundation, audacious angels
from Los Angeles. "Fifty thousand dollars." Impossible.
Awards like this one, when they come, arrive like blizzards
or love, seemingly out of nowhere, a kind of grace. Such gifts
open a whole new realm of imagining. They give the recipient
an audacity of purpose, alter previous self-conceptions, make
the impossible suddenly possible again: house.

That I found the house with ease surprised no one; it was,
of course waiting for me—an 1840 white eyebrow colonial, in
the enchanted, beguiling Hudson Valley. It had everything: a
pond, a smokehouse, a bank of lilies; it was not hard to recognize. Nor was the ghost of the woman who greeted me when I
opened the door. Her joie de vivre, her intelligence, her wit, a
spirit present through the presence of possessions. A Chinese
scroll, a clay bird, a chaise lounge, and in the closet Christmas
ornaments, a kitty-litter box. A dulcimer, a violin in an

unopened violin case—the house had been filled with music
…Schubert on the record player.

I leave her there in winter and begin the long ordeal of
securing a mortgage. The mortgage broker wonders with
some exasperation who will give me a loan as he examines my
"unorthodox employment history," my living from one grant
to the next, a visiting professorship here or there—and me like
a child holding my one golden egg with pride. "It doesn't look
very good," he says, as snow continues to fall. I dream of lilacs
and mountains and Chinese scrolls and snow all jumbled up.
I cling to these things in sleep: the body of a violin shaped like
a small, insistent woman or the rowboat's shape next to the
pond. Having let in the possibility of house, I cannot bear to be
houseless again—and without her. But all winter I cannot see
it; there's too much snow and the house seems suddenly to disappear as fast as it appeared. But Elizabeth is fierce: "Don't
be silly," she whispers, "it's yours now. You deserve it." And
she passes me a ring of shining keys. She's handing them to
me because it's the end of her time here—and the beginning
of mine.

I'd like to sit with her for a minute, safe within the sanctuary of our study, the lilacs like an ocean in the distance, and
just talk, the way you can with those you genuinely admire but
don't really know. I would like to whisper my fears to her, tell
her I dread the impending publication of *The American Woman
in the Chinese Hat.* Tell her I fear the person I was when I wrote
it and know, on any day waking, I might be again. Almost
everyone else is less patient with this sort of thing. They just
want you to get on with it—enjoy your successes, don't worry
so much about the past. But she's more understanding. This
time around at any rate. I am afraid of the person I was then,

so resigned, so desirous of death, I'd tell her. And I imagine she'd say, "I, too, was afraid at times."

She is like the women, starting with my mother, I have tried to keep up with my whole life. You must run breathless just to sit next to them. They prod. They urge. "Look closer; be braver," they say.

Everything of hers is gone now: the dulcimer, the bells, the music she loved preserved on vinyl—all the books. It's okay; she'll grace these halls a long time, I know.

We'll sit until the light is gone. She'll ask if I've found the asparagus patch yet, seen the mockingbird who lives near the mailbox.

She'll wonder how my new work is going. She's stretched out on the chaise lounge, her hand keeping time to some irresistible music. Her beautiful voice drifts through this precious house. She closes her eyes—says she's so happy about the prize —pats my hand, this drowsy angel, already two years dead on the first day we meet, whom I love.

PROVIDENCE, RHODE ISLAND

That nearly perfect lilac-infused existence I am already forced to miss. To in some way already give up.

I am returned to the state of my making. Back to the state of my conception, the very idea of me. Returned to the place of my invention. Home of water and watery memory and pull. I am a little at home. I have come to direct the creative writing program at Brown University. It is perhaps the job that will best allow me to continue doing the writing I need to do. I will only have to teach a little.

I am a wandering soul—but not an aimless one. I've learned well how to listen and I've gone wherever my work told me to go. Wherever my work took me, insistent, I went. I have been forced, in order to continue writing on my own terms, to leave over and over again. I who live everywhere and nowhere have built a home of language. I have been forced to create a home of my own making. A home of music and desire. I can at this point make a home wherever I go. I open my large artist's notebook, I pick up a pen, I turn on the radio; I dream of you —the best, the most mysterious one, the most remote and beautiful aspect of self.

The necessity to find ways to continue, without for the most part the luxury of financial reward, has made it imperative to imagine a home that might be moveable. It has had to be okay to live outside familiarity, outside comfort, outside anything that seems mine. All along I have found it necessary to live with a home that can be conjured within.

Home might be a studio in a loft in Tribeca, a room in Provincetown, an office in Normal, Illinois. Home is anywhere my mind catches fire, my body. Where language trembles and burns.

I am at work now on several projects—a book of rage called *Defiance,* a book of desire: *The Erotic Etudes.* And *The Bay of Angels,* of course. The continued exploration of the possibilities of language is the only real life I know, the only place I've lived truly, fully, all these years. I have spent fifteen years of devotion at the altar of the impossible. I've spent fifteen years building my unshakable home of language and love. The place of longing and failure (for who could succeed?) where I live recklessly, without concern for the product, or the consequences, or the future. My house of yearning and mystery and peace. A place of grace. My mother praying for a child to be born, to come to term, and another mother singing French songs—and the war. And in the étude I've just finished—a woman on a bridge, dressed in white, dipping her hands into the sacred Ganges—it is and is not me. One lives in awe, next to the silence and the strangeness as the lost or hidden or forgotten aspects of self and world, only glimpsed at, are sensed, if only a little. In the challenge, I am at home. In concentration I feel at ease—pure pleasure, pure joy, as I have not experienced in any other way.

After a week of interviews, readings, anxieties, stresses of all sorts—no time to write—I finally can get back a little to some work on *Defiance.* Having been away, disoriented, without anchor, and coming back, I write the line, "Who will mind my savage goat and pole dog?" and this arrangement of words makes me feel more calm, more relieved, more at home than I have felt in some time. Why? Why does this sentence have such an effect over me? It is because a sentence like that completely embodies in language all of my anxiety and frustration and uncertainty and rage—it is an awkward sentence, strange, off-balance, precarious. Darkly imagined, it seems to break off from the body of the rest of the text it is a part of, to assume an eerie and haunting independence. A splintered, troubling thing. It so captures my emotional state *in language* that I am no longer so alone, marooned in it: the emotional state is approximated through the physicality of language, mirrored, and as a result becomes company, something present, something palpable.... The language construct is no longer *about* an emotional state for me, but has become one, and in that way I am no longer utterly isolated in it and without a viable structure. Home is any ordinary, gorgeous sentence that is doing its work.

Home for me is in the syntax, in the syllables. In the syncopations and in the silences. A movement in the mind, the eye, the mouth. Home is the luminous imagination. India haunting me after the Satyatjit Ray retrospective. Home is in Sappho's fragments, in imagining what was there before the papyrus tore. The imagination providing a foundation, a roof, and windows that let you see forever.

The glowing imagination. The place in the distance, amidst the maelstrom of the blizzard toward which "poets will walk without thinking, as if walking home," as Tsvetaeva has said. That place, distant, mysterious, ever-fleeting, changing and shifting, but glimmering in the distance.

Home is that drugged, seductive other state—creation not so unlike the dark, sexual descent. Now a house burns on the page. Now I am in flames. This is the aim of my erotic études: to explore those relationships between language and desire, my sacred, twinned notions of home. In this alternate place, this other reality, outside, apart from one's other life (having moved again, having left, been displaced, been hurt, been diminished and forced to operate in a world so unlike one's real world). A state so deeply meditative, so deeply sexual, so like music. Home is still the music drifting. My parents whispering. The precious alphabet she taught me. And her lovely body. Home is the bodies of women: safe. And all the songs they sang— and sing.

One afternoon while I am dreaming *Defiance,* I finally realize, I know, yes, the little girl Bernadette and Fergus, her older brother, will go fishing—that is it—and somehow it all falls into its proper balance: austere, mysterious, impossibly simple and elegant. Yes, that is it. And I am completely elated and then serene. As happy as I have ever been. Who would not choose to live there?

When I write sentences I am at home. When I make shapes. When I do not, I am damned, doomed, homeless; I know this well—restless, roaming; the actual places I've lived become unrecognizable, and I, too, monstrous, am unrecognizable to myself. In the gloating, enormous strangeness and solitude of the real world, where I am so often inconsolable, marooned, utterly dizzied—all I need do is to pick up a pen and begin to write—safe in the shelter of the alphabet, and I am taken home. Back into the blinding waves, the topaz light, the fire. Or far off into the enthralling, voluptuous dark.

The child draws the letter A.

*She closes her eyes and is surprised to see Matisse
sitting on his balcony in Nice, looking at a woman,
a bird, a hat, some fish in a bowl, turning them over
and over in search of serenity, until he sees a pattern
finally, turning them over until they glow.*

Miracles might occur...

Movement and stasis:

We took the overnight train.

You kissed me everywhere.

A beautiful, passing landscape. Imagined in the dark.

Notes of a Lyric Artist
Working in Prose:

A LIFELONG CONVERSATION
WITH MYSELF ENTERED MIDWAY

*A*N EROTIC song cycle.

AVA could not have been written as it was, I am quite sure, if I
had not been next to the water day after day. Incorporating the
waves.

Making love those afternoons at dusk, just as the shapes were
taken back. Afterwards darkness. Provincetown in winter.

The design of stars then in the sky. I followed their dreamy
instructions. Composed in clusters. Wrote constellations of
associations.

Loving the world, and needing it, as I did. Wanting to trans-
mute it into shapes. Begging it to—

"Stay a little."

Virginia Woolf: "The idea has come to me that what I want to do now is to saturate every atom. I mean to eliminate all waste, deadness, superfluity: to give the moment whole; whatever it includes....It must include nonsense; fact; sordidity; but made transparent."

The desire of the novel to be a poem. The desire of the girl to be a horse. The desire of the poem to be an essay. The essay's desire, its reach towards fiction. And the obvious erotics of this.

Virginia Woolf knew the illusion of fiction is gradual even if moments are heart-stopping, breathtaking. There is a pattern, which is only revealed as patterns are, through elongation and perspective, the ability to see a whole, a necklace of luminous moments strung together. How to continue the progression, the desire to go beyond the intensity of the moment or of moments. Like sex, one has to figure out how to go on after the intensity of the moment—how in effect to compose a life afterwards, how to conjure back a world worth living in, a world which might recall, embrace the momentary, glowing, obliterating, archetypal. One longs for everything. For the past one never experienced, for the future one will never know—except through the imaginative act. One longs to be everything. To have everything.

A certain spaciousness. There would be time and room for it all.

The creation of an original space. The desire for an original space in which to work.

Passion of the mind. Persistent desire for form to meld with idea and emotion in organic ways.

Restlessness of the form. *Every rose pulses.*

Gertrude Stein: "It can easily be remembered that a novel is everything."

Accuse me again, if you like, of over-reaching.

The novel's capacity for failure. Its promiscuity, its verve. Always trying to attain the unattainable. Container of the uncontainable. Weird, gorgeous vessel. Voluptuous vessel.

Room for the random, the senseless, the heartbreaking to be played out. A form both compressed, distilled, and expansive enough to accommodate the most difficult and the most subtle states of being.

Musings, ideas, dreams, segues, shifts in key, athletic feats of imagination, leaps and swirls. Or small, nearly imperceptible progresses. The unarticulated arc of our lives.

Many fiction writers do not, I believe, acknowledge reality's remoteness, its mysteriousness. Its inaccessibility to us and to our modes of expression, though the novel is one of the very few good places for this sort of exploration.

Together, many novelists, now commodity makers, have agreed on a recognizable reality, which they are all too happy to impart as if it were true. Filled with hackneyed ways of perceiving, clichéd, old sensibilities, they and the publishing houses create traditions which have gradually been locked into place. They take for granted: the line, the paragraph, the chapter, the story, the storyteller, character.

I love most what the novel might be, and not what it all too often is.

Reach.

The novel as a kind of eternity. A kind of infinity. Inevitable progressions of beauty—with room and time enough for it all.

Not to worry.

Lyrical novels imply a formal design—an aesthetic patterning in order to achieve the desired intensity.

A personal sensibility projected through the minds and actions of others so that both the lyric and the narrative might be achieved. The lyric self coupled with the novelist's "omniscient" visions.

My relationship to poetry was always one of reverence: How could I ever approach such beauty, such perfection? An unhealthy relationship, finally. With fiction I feel far less reverent. What has been done? Maybe not that much.

The novel might be musically or visually conceived—pictorial relationships, symphonic turns rendered in prose.

The novel's design, for me, being an abstract relationship between parts.

Recognition of the patterns, the relationships, so they might be destroyed if necessary or deviated from or tampered with.

The ability to manipulate shapes and space. Writing *AVA* I felt at times more like a choreographer working with language in physical space. Language, of course, being gesture and also occupying space. Creating relations which exist in their integrity for one fleeting moment and then are gone, remaining in the trace of memory. Shapes that then regather and re-form, making for their instant, new relations, new longings, new recollections, inspired by those fleeting states of being.

Complexities.

How to prolong the lyric moment?

Andrey Tarkovsky: "Writing which links images through the linear, rigidly logical development of plot...usually involves arbitrarily forcing them into sequence in obedience with some abstract notion of order. And even when this is not so, even when plot is governed by characters, one finds that the links which hold it together rest on a facile interpretation of life's complexities."

Room as well for the random, the accidental, and the associations and shapes that arise from allowing accidents to happen.

It's not easy to keep this thing from that. At other times I feel most like a composer. More than anything else I aspire to the state of music. It's not desirable or possible to keep things separate. Many things arise:

The child draws the luminous letter A.

As a girl my favorite novel was *Wuthering Heights*. But I could not find a book anywhere else remotely like it. It created a hunger.

And my father playing his trumpet. Lying in the dark listening to that aching music. And how it seemed to approximate all we could not say.

Always I have loved poetry most, but at the same time felt the need for a larger canvas: a series of panels, a series of screens.

My form is always an odd amalgam—taken from painting, sculpture, theory, film, music, poetry, dance, mathematics— even fiction sometimes.

Reread: Goethe's *Werther,* Hölderlin's *Hyperion,* Gide's *Le Voyage d'Urien,* Barnes's *Nightwood,* Melville's *Moby Dick.*

To sit next to the great mysteries, or to lie in the dark next to them and find shapes, ephemeral and changing as they may be, for this. All this:

A beautiful passing landscape.

Our uncertainties, hopes, fears, longings, disappointments, our forgetfulness. Our relationship to language.

Huddled around the fire of the alphabet.

A free and large enough notion of story so that it does not coerce. All too often novels are narratives of coercion because they are too narrowly conceived.

A novel presumes a story and a storyteller. But who is the self who is telling? And what is the story? And where have we gotten our small definitions of story? And why?

And what if the story is:

The way you sound in letters, or on the beach, or at the moment of desire.

Three P.M. when the shadows cross the border.

The way you looked that night on your knees.

The way the swing swung.

And if not the real story, then what the story was for me.

The pull and drag of the tide.

Gertrude Stein: "I have destroyed sentences and rhythms and literary overtones and all the rest of that nonsense, to get to the very core of this problem of communication of intuition. If the communication is perfect the words have life, and that is all there is to good writing, putting down on the paper words which dance and weep and make love and fight and kiss and perform miracles."

To use all and everything that is available to us through observation, memory, fantasy, desire, imagination—so as to get up close next to one's vision.

Miracles might occur.

Jean-Luc Godard: "Cinema is not a series of abstract ideas but rather the phrasing of moments."

New definitions of story and character may be required. To imagine story as a blooming flower or a series of blossomings. To change the narrative drive, to better mimic one's own realities, drives. So that narrative might be many things. *One hundred love letters, written by hand.*

Understand and accept the limitations and contours of the traditional narrative. In *The American Woman in the Chinese Hat,* my third novel (published fourth), there is an end to narrative as I once understood it. Without going there first, I do not believe I could have gotten to *AVA*—which is something quite else.

And characters may be perceived as a light or a force or a pressure, or as an aspect of possibility.

In the negotiations between poetry and prose one might like something neater. Let's put our mind to it:

To each—both lyrical fiction and poetry, a certain irresistible music. An Orphic voice speaking. A childish belief in the whole.

Is the sustaining of the lyric voice (certainly a kind of stamina) dependent on an insistent and pervasive sexuality? One feels an intimate link between the two.

The desire for—

Miracles.

Miracles. Helen reading my father the recipe for ravioli dough. He remembers his family drying pasta on all the beds in the Brooklyn house of his childhood. "Dig a well. Then put in eggs." And I type it directly into the text of *AVA,* which I am working on in the next room. A place for the random, the accidental, the overheard, the incidental. *Precious, disappearing things.*

"Stay a little."

I love you.

An expansive narrative. Bela Tarr's *Sátántangó*—a terrifying film, filled with exhilarating narrative choices.

In my new work I want music, meditation, narrative, philosophy, more—and all at once.

I give myself room. The drama of the creative imagination being my one true subject. A continuous exploration made concrete, somewhat palpable, through fiction.

My aim in *The American Woman in the Chinese Hat* was to dramatize the breakdown of language, and with that carrying off of language, a belief system, a world. Much of the book's drama is linguistic. The novel, being a spacious form, allowed me to establish the rules of language within a temporal framework and then, once established and understood, I could subvert them. This is one of the things novels do well. The world falls apart as you read. One hopes, by the end that the impact of the fractures are not only understood, but felt. Because having been engaged, involved in the fluency of images, when they begin to dissolve, one feels dissolved as well. Only shards remain, disrupted syntax, words detached from their meanings. A bleak code calling up the lost, the fluent, the integrated world, once whole. Language enacts the speed and degree and manner of breakdown. We are forced to witness an entire history: a world is born, evolves, warps and finally breaks. Breakdown is dramatized, imaginative and linguistic ways of escape are cut off.

She hears a high sound. Like mermaids or birds. She's watching her hat. Strange angel. Butterfly.

To lose fluency. To become speechless.

The choice of lyrical techniques must augment and enhance the narrative decisions. Only then will the result be radiant, authentic, inevitable, grave.

Tarkovsky: "I think in fact that unless there is an organic link between the subjective impressions of the author and his objective representation of reality, he will not achieve even superficial credibility, let alone authenticity and inner truth."

Much of my work is propelled by the desire to be reunited with lost, unremembered aspects of self and world.

Who were we, and why did we live?

Aspects of self, aspects of personality, temperament, take an outward shape and then are animated. Often, my obsessions, fears, hopes, all that matters most, grow heads, arms, legs and then move, interact with one another, in the form of characters.

Character, rather than well-rounded carriers of story, might work more like images do.

She waves. Wavers. In the agony of the afternoon. In a red dress. The American Woman in the Chinese Hat. She's not American at all. She is German maybe, or Suedoise. And she has no hat.

Poetry and prose. How to reconcile poetic forms with the narrative requirements of an extended prose work? Because finally, yes, it is the novel I have to work in.

A new energy is needed to sustain a contemporary lyric fiction. The energy of writing into one's desires, passion. The energy derived from many things might sustain such a voice. The energy from writing outside of fashion, against the fictive fashion, even. Easy to be a renegade in such an inauspicious fiction milieu. Use it to your advantage.

How to prolong the lyric moment?

What might the phrasing of moments look like in prose?

Rent Godard's *Pierrot le Fou.*

The novelist's lyric "I" engaged, as the epic poet is, in the world. A singer singing *in relation to* others. This perhaps defines the difference of the enterprise between lyric novelist and lyric poet.

The novel as huge, shifting, unstable, unmanageable canvas. Smudged with lipstick, fingerprints, crumpled, tear-stained, many-paged.

The novel as a geometry of desire.

A high sound like burning... Stranger. Light. The sound of water over stones. She waves. Each word in its watery globe. Pulses. Once, twice, good-bye. Love. Forever. A woman. Floating like a heart. And roses.

How to prolong the lyric moment?

In *The American Woman with the Chinese Hat,* the reiteration and gradual mutation of images mirror the disintegrating psyche of a narrator in the process of mental breakdown. The novel makes this acting out possible.

In a lyric novel, objects often are emanations of the unconscious.

I love winter most because it's the most recognizable outward correlation I know of my interior life. There is recognition. *Snow falls like music.*

What is narrative? Narrative might be:
I wrote you one hundred love letters.
One thousand love letters, written by hand.
This is probably the last love letter I will ever write.
One thousand love letters—you probably never got them all.

Prose, it seems to me, has the great ability to *dramatize* states of mind, as well as incorporating other kinds of "action" and development.

In *AVA* though there are elements of story everywhere, I am still reluctant and unprepared to say what the story is.

A polyphony. A bouquet of voices.

The storyteller as chameleon. Fluid, mutable.

The novel is all potential. All what might be. All what might have been. A record of all we cannot remember, all we've lost—never to be retrieved.

Despite my efforts, it resists me, eludes me. Perhaps it might be possible to write a perfect poem, but I do not believe it is possible, or even desirable, to write the perfect novel. That is what I love most about the form.

It is as rebellious, as unruly as I am.

There is another kind of novel other than the novel of adventure, the novel of manners, the psychological, the realist novel. It is strange, exotic, hybrid—and it is beautiful.

Lyrical fiction introduces the conventions of poetry (image, metaphor) into a genre dependent on causation and time. Characters, scenes, plots are turned into patterns, designs of imagery. Life and manners are sensually apprehended and then turned into design.

Lyrical novels are concerned with aesthetic relations—space, temporal and shape relations, tone and tempo. They are sensitive to tensions and pulls, resistances—gatherings and release.

An imaginative act, a design in which life is simultaneously brought up close and also viewed from afar at a more detached distance.

As in my *The American Woman in The Chinese Hat,* where figs, roses, butterfly, angel, fire, floating, stranger, red achieve a measure of impersonality, universality, love, dread. Inner emotion transforms the outer world into a fever dream, a hallucination where images from the exterior world are thrust into strange, glowing relief and reflect both a verisimilitude, a portrait of the outer world as we can know it, and a private, interior, symbolic reality.

This sort of work requires a strange combination of both utter control and complete recklessness.

A leaping and staying in one place at the same time. Paradoxically what is closest and most personal is also turned into the universal, outside and removed from the self. Abstract and concrete at the same time.

Characters, too, weave patterns. Voices overlap as do motifs, echoing one another, reiterating, enlarging. Many techniques are employed: call and response, rubato, counterpoint, and these strategies heighten and formalize the ordinary narrative ploys.

The Waves by Woolf to my mind being the precursor to my *AVA*. Symbolic qualities are felt, perceived through voice and rhythm. Whole worlds are conjured in scraps of dialogue, a turn of the head, a pause, a deletion, a last extravagance. One feels, if I've been at all successful, their colors, tones, pressures, their human presences.

There is compression in lyric fiction, yes, but also expansion. Elongation. The longing for clearings. An opening up of perceptions, possibilities, every time the writer or the reader sits down. And duration, and the obvious erotics of this.

How to reconcile succession of time and sequence, of cause and effect, with the instantaneous moments of the lyric?

Tarkovsky: "All must come from inner necessity, from an organic process. Any artificial move is easily detected."

Reread Poe, Novalis.

Is the loss of self in lyrical fiction like the loss of self in poetry?

One thing is evident: the conventional psychological novel with its phony or simplistic truisms and its grasping at straws doesn't approximate experience sufficiently.

Portraits of the mind and the moves the mind makes.

And if not the real story, then—

A girl in a striped bathing suit sits at the water's edge. She digs deeply in the sand and from the vast beach makes shapes: an arch, a pyramid, two towers.

And if not the real story, then what the story was for me.

A feminine shape—after all this time.

Virginia Woolf in "Modern Fiction" (1919) criticizes Joyce's *Ulysses* for not ever going beyond the self. And this is always my problem, too, with Joyce, and why for me he fails finally to be a great novelist.

Not to own or colonize or dominate.

The known world dissolves into feelings and groups of feelings, into music, which then might escape the dilemma, the trap of the personal.

Perversely, I find Joyce too confining.

To sing in prose, to somehow get the urgency of bone and blood and hair, entire histories, into prose.

Prose which remains lyrical in intention eschews consecutive action for other kinds of narratives. The narratives are not merely associative either; it's rather more mysterious and elusive.

The identification of self and world transmuted into shapes.

Virginia Woolf's "Mr. Bennett and Mrs. Brown."

In Woolf I think more than any other writer the conventions of the novel blend most perfectly with poetic technique.

The narrative beliefs that animated and propelled with such authority writers like Jane Austen no longer hold. Writers are forced into a reexamination of what are useable forms, if they are serious writers. What forms might be opened up by our particular predicament. This is a poetic as well as a fictive concern.

Woolf writes in "How it Strikes a Contemporary" that twentieth-century writers "cannot make a world, cannot generalize. They cannot tell stories because they do not believe that stories are true."

As we try to make meaning—

The shattered glass might mend.

—where maybe there is none.

Woolf implies that the writer may have to write notebooks rather than masterpieces. Notes instead of coherent, authoritarian, beginning-middle-and-end, thesis-and-conclusion pieces.

Virginia Woolf from *The Writer's Diary:* "The idea has come to me that what I want now to do is to saturate every atom. I mean to eliminate all waste, deadness, superfluity: to give the moment whole; whatever it includes. Say that the moment is a combination of thought, sensation, the voice of the sea…It must include nonsense; fact; sordidity; but made transparent."

The problem of course is that a sequence of illuminations is simply not enough.

A kind of liberation, a freedom, occurs by assuming the concentrating and illumination, the saturation of the moment as in poetry; and the prolonged temporal ability to stay where one's vision is and watch it evolve, change, double back on itself, augment, amplify, come to uneasy terms, resolutions—of a sort, as extended prose is capable of doing.

A poetic unity. An ecstatic, even mystical, integrity.

What is perhaps most astounding is the typical novelist's almost total disregard for language, as if it were only some bothersome means to an end. Some way of imparting information. And most prose called "poetic" is turgid, purplish, overwrought, self-conscious.

An intimate knowledge of the workings of language is as essential for prose writers as it is for poets. No matter what sort of fiction one writes.

The external world, facts, history, politics, manners, and the natural world shall be embraced. Also dreams, loves, fears—all aspects of the interior life.

Symphonic forms. Fugue forms. The improvisations of jazz. Montage. Jump cuts. Slow dissolves. Cubism, Cortázar, abstraction, the troubadours, the left-handed child. Love songs.

Woolf in *The Common Reader*: Forget that "appalling narrative business of the realist: getting from lunch to dinner."

Jane Austen ended forever a certain tradition. Reread Austen, Balzac, and all those you made facile enemies of back when you were struggling for a vision, for a voice. She had taken a certain kind of novel to its limits. I needed, I suppose, as a result to demonize her. Had no room for her.

We have witnessed the demise of the belief system that made Jane Austen's confidence and coherence possible.

In Chicago, I step into a small foyer before entering the magnificent lobby. It has been designed this way so we might feel and experience the space, the grandeur. The architect understood this. The novelist could well benefit from becoming an architect in prose.

The question persists: can poetic insight ever truly be reconciled with the novel's form? On the side of narrative—a plot of motives, time, and causality. Poetry—image and pattern.

The attempt in *AVA* is that narrative motifs might produce a design of images. To interweave motifs through the text by use of recurrences, repetitions, etc., which often act contrapuntally and trigger through theme, rhythm, and other mysterious methods associations in the reader as well as the writer. Often it is the act itself, the association-making process rather than the subject, that is recognizable.

My favorite literature, that which really lives for me, is always an experience in itself: a drama of language and shape and rhythms, and not just the record of an experience.

That language is feeling. That syntax is feeling. One should feel in one's whole being the necessity and inevitability of tense, point of view, tempo, voice, etc. That where the paragraph breaks is not taken for granted. That the notion of chapter is not taken for granted.

And that the formal patterns not constrict. Ephemeral, imperfect, stories without their old authority. "Notebooks" maybe "rather than masterpieces."

Somewhere around seventh grade it seemed everyone was killing themselves or being killed. I was often afraid. Jimi Hendrix. Janis Joplin. RFK. Martin Luther King. The desire of the girl to be a horse. To run away or save. Save anyone. Just once.

The brother draws the letter K. The mother guides his hand. Says: *try*. Says: *you can*.

To use scenes, to ask scenes to function as image. I think unconsciously this was what I was trying in my first novel, *Ghost Dance*. So that scene by scene it makes the kinds of leaps that poetry makes line by line.

How to get character to function as image without contrivance. Time as character.

To witness the unfolding of the imagination across time and space. Like the sun rising on the bay. Provincetown in winter.

As we walk through plane after symbolic plane. In *The American Woman in the Chinese Hat* the fountain, the roses, the figs, the light, the forever.

In *The American Woman in the Chinese Hat* to find the formal arrangement of words in that limited and constantly diminishing set of possibilities that might save both protagonist and author. The struggle enacted on a formal plane.

Each word a fig.

After all the betrayals.

To orchestrate color in *The American Woman in the Chinese Hat:* pink and sea-green drinks, yellow drinks, a poet in a white dress, a young Arlesian in a bright blue robe, like hope —and then to systematically drain the world of every color— except red.

Vin rosé, Cotes du Rhône—so many roses, and a red dress.

A red-drenched ending.

To take one to the point of no return—and then somehow, I don't know how, to return.

Fidelity to one's perceptions. Trust. *We look out the window at the red sign that says PSYCHIC.*

One of the direct challenges of poetry is to make language work again. Something fiction, although it is made of language, tends to relegate almost always to the basement. To be responsive and responsible to thought, to emotion, to the body, in language.

Poetry to my mind rejects habitual thinking far more readily than fiction. There seems less reverence for the accepted, the tired, the cherished gestures and forms. Fiction, too often, has substituted plot for structure. Fiction writers must be structuralists in order to realize the potential of the novel or the story, but for the most part they are not.

Only now and then, I realize, do I get anywhere close to a real insight, anywhere near. As usual, I grope in the dark. Aim at the thing.

The ultimate trust. To let go in the dark.

Not to fear being ludicrous. Not to fear failing magnificently. Like the films of Kieslowski, for example. Walk the fine line between being simply preposterous and utterly convincing.

Not to protect oneself. Expose your heart. Your circular, flawed, contradictory thought process, your hopes, ambitions, vulnerabilities.

To write risking ridicule. To risk being ridiculous, inappropriate, over the top. *Defiance* will be such a project.

Fiction might allow miracles to arise in the luxury of its space and time. It has the capacity to dramatize interior states. To dramatize longing, to dramatize distance.

As a girl when she was sad she would turn herself into a horse. Her left-handed brother. He's very sick.

I don't remember the knife from before, the American woman says near the end to the young Arlesian—*or your blood red robe.*

Every rose pulses.

In a novel far away longings can be quite literally far. The text can mirror, approximate, distance. The text can incorporate longing through its formal structures. It can make tentative approaches or bold, operatic gestures. It can enact reunion. It can double back on itself, revise itself, simulate larger postponements, resignations. Incorporate giddiness, dizziness, lust, love even. All this is possible in the novel's structure.

Music often performs similar feats. But the novel is different in that it conveys literal meanings simultaneous to the meaning it conveys through form and through the color and timbre and rhythms of language.

Miracles might arise.

The permission to make peace, forgive, admit when you've been wrong. The permission to be afraid.

My friend who makes glass books, far away, calls to say—

I look out at my spring garden. Hear the pulsing rose of her heart.

One might stop time for awhile…

But a series of radiant tableaux are not enough.

A healing, a suturing, a reconciliation…everything having been broken, or taken away.

The dream all along: to be free.

There will be room and time for everything. This will include missteps, mistakes, speaking out of turn. Amendments, erasures, illusions. The creation of a kind of original space will mean:

Everything I ever wanted was there. Everything I ever feared or desired. Yes, time and place enough for everything. I've come closest to this, thus far, in *AVA*.

A place where there would be time and opportunity enough to turn old hierarchies on their heads. A place to re-imagine epiphany.

And if not the real story, then what the story was for me.

Mallarmé's "Le Nenuphar Blanc." Each image devolving until all that is left is the pure, white strangeness of the water lily.

I don't remember the knife from before, or your blood red robe.

She remembers the little emperor and how his hands turned the water red. Rose trout. She slept with a girl with crimson hair once. Objects are emanations of the subconscious. As in poetry there is a juxtaposition of themes and motifs. A manipulation of sound. Sound as desire.

Ava Klein in my *AVA* on the last day of her life with her one last late hope: Chinese herbs. World traveler, she had wanted to see China. This longing called up as she swallows one tablet after the next. She may have had lovers there, friends: Shi Sun, Steve Ning, Victor Chang. A line of beautiful boys—which recalls her friend Aldo, an opera singer, dead of AIDS, and his beautiful boys. Chinese tablets, China, Chinese boys, a poem: (She was a lover of literature, a professor of literature and desire.) Healing herbs, the healing lines of a poem by an ancient and forgotten poet. The one thousand Chinese murdered in a square. The desire to heal them. And all those who have been murdered. Her family in Treblinka, the whole universe, the breaking heart of the world. "The desire to speak in a language that heals as much as it separates," as Hélène Cixous says. And maybe this after all is narrative.

And if not the real story—

The ability to embrace oppositional stances at the same time. Contradictory impulses, ideas, motions. To assimilate as part of the form, incongruity, ambivalence.

To make a place for ambivalence or uncertainty to be *experienced* and not just referred or alluded to seems one of the most interesting challenges of the novel. The tentative, the unresolved, the incomplete might be enacted. Played out in the theater of one's imagination.

The potential for celebration. Exuberance. Virtuosity. Joy.

What did you think was beautiful there?

The intricate pattern on the scarf on the head of a Yugoslavian woman is beautiful, and the way you tried to hide your disappointment at not winning the prize so as not to spoil the evening is beautiful. And the small bird as it arrives elegantly on the plate. And how surely if I have loved anyone it is you. And how you understood in the end why we could not make it work, despite love— despite everything we had going.

I have come to celebrate. I have come to praise.

The American Woman in the Chinese Hat for me is a novel of black celebration, a riot of language and exhaustion and despair. *AVA* on the other hand is a novel of bright celebration, of coming together, of all possibilities, of joy, jouissance.

Ecstatic dancing to klezmer and nonsense texts.

As lyric as *The American Woman in the Chinese Hat* is, as patterned, as dependent on image and design, the book would not work in a shorter or more truncated form. It could not work even as a long poem. A novel of loss, told simultaneously with hothouse vibrancy and an odd, detached, cool ferocity, it could not have approximated loss without first suggesting and then suggesting again and again through the fictive conventions of narrative, what exactly was at stake.

We were working on an erotic song cycle. It was called: *Everything I Owned.* Everything I loved or wanted or feared was here.

To be fierce, strict, smart, like Woolf. Woolf thought Meredith created figures of large, universal, elemental structure, but that these characters lacked concreteness and depth. They were too general to be collective. The qualities of both poetry and prose simultaneously must be achieved by the lyric novelist. The poet novelist must also measure up as a novelist; yes, how silly, of course. Few are up to this. And yet it is crucial, of great importance.

Stein: "Who can think about a novel. I can."

Themes in *The American Woman in the Chinese Hat* are reiterated, expanded, echoed as part of the plan, and in this way very dependent on song: "Row, row, row your boat...life is but a dream." It is not a casual reference, as nothing in this kind of work can be casual—but rather speaks again and again to what is happening in the narrator's psyche. The transformation of Catherine's psychic world is constantly mirrored in the outside world. Each word is a boat, a small saving thing in this increasingly dark, blood-drenched dream. Sea.

Language engenders language. Language itself presents unexpected and often extraordinary solutions. It leads you to the what next? To the how and why. To the *what if*, and *if only*.

Think about Camus, Malraux, Sarraute, Robbe-Grillet.

Throughout, images such as boats, dream, figs, swans, roses, horses, gloating, angel, butterfly endlessly repeat themselves in varying configurations as the imagination gropes and tries to make sense of chaotic experience. As the imagination tries to save, the outward world distorts to speak of the interior world. The internal world informs the external one. A hallucination. A fever dream. The way often of prose poems, I think.

Reread Baudelaire's prose poems.

There's a kind of glittering out there—a dark aching, a long-ing that can only be adequately felt through form. In *The American Woman in the Chinese Hat* for instance, tentative ges-tures give way over time to inevitability. The move towards a radiant place, a place of rigorous disintegration, a place the architecture of the novel allows and makes possible.

And all day pretty girls dip their arms like swans into the foun-tain...

The dark swan of her desire floating out into the pool...

At the cemetery flowers float in their watery globes...

You said: swans. He can't help but see swans now at the fountain...

The search still remains, after all this time, (the search that was *The Art Lover's* search, 1985–1989) in finding a language in which to speak and the forms that might approximate.

All this:

Forever. For the languages of star and ash and music and numbers. The search for the blue flower of poetry, or a red dress.

As we mimic the heartbeat in our upright walk, home.

Someone puts on Madame Butterfly in the square and they cry.

Woolf: "Stand at the window and let your rhythmical sense open and shut, boldly and freely until one thing melts into another, until the taxis are dancing with the daffodils, until a whole has been made from all the separate fragments."

How to get it even a little right:

My mother whispering in the next room during the years of my childhood. She's worried about my brother again. He's got a hole in his heart. He's very sick. And on the television now Bosnia. And floating in that room *won't die*. How do winds, the first crocuses (I'll bring them to my teacher), the passage of stars, of time—that's Orion's belt; what Mrs. Smith is calling out across the yard (sounds like bar talk) and birdsong. The body next to mine in bed, warmth and then warmth gone away. Where? To work? To the store? What year is it? Mrs. Smith said, *it's Bartok*. I hear the music now she's playing for me and her daughter Alison. The cuckoos when I finally got to France sounded just like that clock. For a moment it is the room of my childhood, three girls in the same bedroom, the cuckoo clock. Another baby, maybe on the way. *No!* I say emphatically and then traffic—the apartment in New York. On the television, the weatherman. The girl picks up the magic book and reads it at night by flashlight. That's me; of course.

The illusion of including, of having it all. So many desires. A mélange of influences, techniques, pressures.

As a child my favorite book was the poetic, mystical *Wuthering Heights*. A somber, lonely, ecstatic meditation. So much solitude in the midst of everything. Three girls in the bedroom. Many children. So much going on. Why was I always so lonely? And still am. In the midst of much joy, such estrangement. How to get some of that down right.

As I take what I perceive, what I see out there, and abstract it, returning with a coherence, a solace of form, a shape.

The challenge: To turn the world, and the workings of the world, into song.

I love the things that continue. That never end. I love the long haul. Is this the novelist's disposition? The forever.

The ancient consoling tradition. The impulse to sing. The impulse to tell a story, to want to know insatiably, at times, what happens next.

That said, I must admit that conventional storytelling bores me silly. The analytic bits, the dreary descriptive impulse, the cause and effect linearity, the manufactured social circumstances.

To create whole worlds through implication, suggestion, in a few bold strokes. Not to tyrannize with narrative. Allow a place for the reader to live, to dream.

All of sex called up in an apartment vestibule. All reckless, incandescent desire. As in illuminated manuscripts, an emblematic approach to narrative.

Careful of the intercom.

Now in America they call this coffee, but I remember coffee. Let the reader linger there. Go where she will.

The novel is something, even when stopped, which is continuous.

I wanted to be obliterated by light, stunned, dazzled, stopped, and also to never die. To go on.

Each word a boat.

I wanted in my books prayers, bells, arabesques, dervishes, a doomed blood, a remote chorus, the static of cats, the way you looked that night, turning away—modulations to other keys. I wanted it all: the moment and the elongation of the moment, and then another moment, and the cumulative pleasures of an intensifying, building content. I was greedy. I believed it might all be possible.

Not to forget the lost songs of the troubadours and the unfixed relationship between words and music. A way in prose perhaps of speaking to some of my extraordinary solitude?

To fail. To miss the mark. To not even come close.

In the midst of ecstatic possibility, sometimes, even then, no way out.

No longer the hunger for figs. The hunger for an arrangement of anything.

Shattering of glass.

Rilke's *Malte Laurids Brigge* is like my *American Woman* in that both, as lyric novels, move image by image toward intensity. Images follow a progress through interplays and modulation until they reach a level of nearly unbearable intensity. Action is a concern, but a secondary one.

The beauty and terror of silence intrigues me. Poetry reveres silence. Fiction too often tries to fill it up. And sound, voluptuous, reinsisting itself against that backdrop of silence, takes on a different quality.

As we form our first words after making love.

Not to take anything for granted.

But digression seems more built into the potential of the novel. Is true digression more possible in fiction, in that one may completely forget one strand of reality, having replaced it by an equally compelling and lengthy one, which might wipe out for awhile, obliterate what has preceded it? And then to be returned to the first world again, bewildered.

And so we get to the notion of home. The move towards home and the longing called home and all that memory, imagination, desire, belief, doubt can conjure as we circle and circle on this extraordinary journey. The novel filled with acting out, rehearsals, meditations, games from childhood, melancholy rainy afternoons or bright sunlight where you bounced a little ball and picked up glittering stars called jacks in one hand.

Where you bounced a large ball, "A," and you went through the precious alphabet. A my name is Alice. And yes,

It is true my name is Carole Alice.

Perfect the action in your mind that will keep the hula hoop up, or the brother safe, or the dress red.

Allow, because you must allow, the broken glass to speak.

And sometimes when she wasn't sad, but was furious and wanted to get away from all the brothers and sisters, she'd turn herself into a horse.

Time passes: It's shocking. You change shape. Your parents age and eventually die. You remember your mother in a bathing suit, beautiful on a dock at a lake. And when you put on your bathing suit now, she is exactly back at age thirty-five, in you.

Time passes. I digress.

A progress. A child is born. Grows. Learns to write. One day has children. Those children too sing the old songs, teach beloved things to the next children. A progress of numbers. They grow old.

My father playing his trumpet in the moody half-light.

I got to dance in a circle. I got to kiss you on the cheek.

The left-handed boy lived.

I wanted—

The pleasure of accumulated meanings, of accretion, which is the narrative act. A fragile constellation, through time and space, of relationship. An architecture of stars, of—

The joy has been in watching you grow. The joy has been in loving you.

I talk to a faraway friend and ask what will happen next. How did she find out? Who will leave whom? Where did the other woman go? And what about the child? She's not sure. My dear friend, a glass artist, tells me she is making glass books. Will there be further fractures?

One makes shapes.

K.

I wrote you one thousand love letters. You probably never got them all.

I imagine the progress of the glass books as she speaks.

The fragility of her voice trembling over the thin wires.

The relatives place the white ravioli on the beds to dry. I open my mouth to receive the host. Where have you gone?

And when she was joyful as well—she remembers now—ecstatic, she would turn herself into a horse. So that the horse took on many meanings.

The desire of the girl to be a horse. The novel to be a poem. The desire to change shapes again and again.

Is the lyric Orphic voice reliant for its energy and power on an insistent and intense sexuality?

Careful of the intercom.

As I write these notes to myself, I traverse the country "promoting," as they say, my *American Woman in the Chinese Hat.* Right now I am flying from Los Angeles to New York. We're going *fast,* at some 33,000 feet. The nose of the plane is already dipped in night. At the tail, where I sit, last day. This tells me something important, but I don't know what yet, about novel writing. There's movement and stasis. The sun setting at my side.

I'm reading a magazine with Nirvana's Kurt Cobain on the cover in between jotting these things in my notebook. I'm flooded with memories, associations, the history of a lifetime, my lifetime—and these things make Kurt Cobain's suicide even more painful today. Without my points of reference this pain could not exist in this way. The novel can create these responses, these states by the gradual, leisurely building up of moments though space and time. The novel possesses the sound, the structure, the spaciousness, the heart to get some of it down. Let's hope.

Jenny Holzer: "In a dream you saw a way to survive and you were full of joy."

Row your boat, row your small boat.

And, only a little after this it will be Kristen Pfaff, the bass guitarist from the band Hole—good-bye.

My dear glass friend has had a second breast removed now. Now what? Emotion as narrative: sadness, ferocity, fear, can give integrity, as we through fiction rehearse, pray, conjure, bring the night closer and also, simultaneously, dispel it. A beautiful, passing landscape.

Tarkovsky: "The allotted function of art is not, as is often assumed, to put across ideas, to propagate thoughts, to serve as example. The aim of art is to prepare a person for death, to plough and harrow his soul, rendering it capable of turning to good."

How to incorporate the joys and pleasures, tenderness, delicacies, the generosities and seductions of the novel and its narrative capacities with the extraordinary, awesome capabilities of poetry? There's the challenge. Who is up to it? I wonder.

A girl in a striped bathing suit sits at the water's edge. She digs deeply in the sand and from the vast beach makes shapes: an arch, a pyramid, two towers. Not child, but not yet adult, she is at that tender age of becoming.

The glass might mend itself.

The child draws the luminous letter A in the sand. She hears the phosphorescent ocean.

Miracles might occur. Who is up to it?

A small voice rises in me. *I am,* it says.

And then the plane is enveloped in darkness.

For Cynthia
April–December 1994

NOTE: *All italicized material is from a Carole Maso novel or from a work-in-progress.*

Surrender

I HAD COME FROM FRANCE WHERE I had gone to write, living on a borrowed $1,000 for months, but I was at the end of my resources: financial, emotional, psychic. Even this life, beautiful and mysterious and charmed as it was, had become intolerable—I was moving every few weeks, uncertain as to what would happen next, house-sitting or caretaking or other more elaborate and difficult arrangements. And the woman, dear Helen, who had over the years seen me through all this— inventing schemes, guiding me, urging me even into each necessary if troubling arrangement so that it might be possible to write my books—four in all then, in one state or another of completion—she, too, was at her wit's end. And so I had decided to accept, yes, the outlandish, impossible offer of meaningful employment by the wild-eyed iron-willed woman I had met a few years earlier at the MacDowell Colony. She, one Lucia Getsi, had predicted on the first day of my residency there—based on very little, only my first novel—that I would teach at her school, Illinois State University (ISU). With no

MFA, no teaching experience, and no real evidence that the Midwest existed at all, I nodded unworriedly, convinced no such thing would be possible. Two years passed. I went to Provincetown; I went to France; I finished a second novel. But possible indeed it was, and before I knew it Lucia's prediction had come true.

I was destitute, and I had no prospects of publishing. My press, the noble North Point Press, about to do my third book, had just folded, and the New York publishers were less than enthusiastic. What choice did I have? And so once again in sadness, in weariness, my leave-taking began. There had been so many leave-takings already. I would leave France, leave home (New York City), leave Helen, to do a job that I was unconvinced could even be done, in an imaginary Midwest, in a place called Normal.

Landing at the Bloomington, Illinois, airport and looking up into a sky of utter vastness, I felt I was falling upward into a dizzying blue sea. It was captivating here in its vastness, its flatness, its nothingness. I have never seen anything quite like it. Only vaguely does it recall Arles, which Van Gogh thought recalled Holland.

All summer I had walked in lushness, caressed by light, by olive and lemon and fig trees, embraced by gently rolling hills. Because my time in France was coming to its inevitable end, it had become too beautiful there, too painfully perfect. My parting became a kind of unbearable opera of longing. But then, overnight it seemed, there I was in the Midwest, and there was nothing, and the nothingness, the weird, fierce resignation of it was somehow exhilarating. I surrendered in seconds to this void, and like all landscapes I form a permanent bond with, it, at a crucial moment, a moment of crisis, of change, happened to mirror my internal state identically. My remoteness, my desolation. Stepping off that plane, the world was devoid of everything, a clean slate of sky, a nihilism of space, empty, the end, and yet it was oddly beautiful—like my own brand of nihilism.

And so I am dropped headlong into a strange land, a world utterly alien to me: world of dramatic and violent weather, dramatic and resolute landscape, dramatic and bizarre academia. Weird world of students and faculty and politics and paper. I have not been in school for a very many years. And from this vantage point the university seems as odd and coded and impenetrable as just about anything. Because I am just the visiting *artiste,* I do not have to go to faculty meetings, but I do anyway for their circus-like aspects. I go to academic parties for the spectacle, the *Who's Afraid of Virginia Woolf* qualities, the bizarre vocabulary, the accents. I roam Normal/Bloomington memorizing middle America. I am a tourist, and there are many fascinating things out there. I come to class in the first week with my findings. At the hospital down the road I tell them there is a stone bench and engraved into the bench is written, "Today we prepare for our dreams of tomorrow." I tell them as students of writing it's going to be tough going, as they can go and see for themselves, because the clichés are literally written in stone.

In my tour of downtown Bloomington I see a radio tower that looks a lot like the Eiffel Tower. How far I think I've come from anything even a little familiar.

Luckily there are a few new friends: a colleague and fellow fiction writer who murmurs "Blanchot, Blanchot, Blanchot," like a prayer, like the way out of here; another who loves the local band Thrill Kill Cult and Beckett. And of course there is Lucia. Having gotten me into this thing, she takes full responsibility. We swim together several times a week. We take trips to Chicago. She saves me with her thousand generosities: her impromptu three-course Italian meals, her gossip, her poems. Also, she is an extraordinary scholar. She allows me to sit in on her German Romanticism class. She lends me the Novalis translations she has done. It's ecstasy then. Lucia, high-spirited, determined, with her stubborn Tennessee accent, does all she can to cheer me up. She says not to feel so bad—after twenty-five years in Bloomington, she still does not feel at home here.

And there is the woman who the day I arrive has already left five messages on something called the Voice Mail. She implores me to let her enter the class. She is older, about my age. She, too, becomes my friend, with caution, because she is my student, and I know from the first day of class that this is a sacred relationship. It's a delicate balance to maintain, and a crucial one. There are only a few things I tell myself in the beginning: work the students as hard as you work yourself, and respect with your entire being that relationship (in other words, no matter what, do not sleep with them). I am so lonely here. Helen, back in New York, shows no signs whatever of visiting.

In a surprising and unanticipated turn, I end up adoring my students, feel them to be more talented than most of the published writers I have come across, want to celebrate their instincts, their feeling for language, their willingness to try anything with me. They seem unreasonably hopeful, perky, wholesome—but I consider that this may be just in comparison with the French. They are diligent, intelligent, open-minded, and, like the landscape, filled with longing and possibility.

Stupidly and naively and without any real feeling for their

actual lives, I come to class one day thrilled with an event from the evening before—a tornado! The weird, green sky, the awful silence, the seemingly backward-flying birds. I tell them of my fantasy: to go to the thing's center, to be obliterated, to achieve oblivion. In reality when the tornado comes I have no idea what to do and feel scared. No key to the basement, I stay in my attic apartment alone, the radio saying over and over, take cover. I'm afraid—and there's no one here to die with me. The class is clearly appalled by my comments. What do I know of the grief such phenomena have caused them, their families? Immediately I regret my flippant tourism. The next day I go into a brief but heartfelt apology. I have learned something. What was I thinking? After my apology they slowly begin to trust me. They tell me about cows and corn and the prairie. The semester can begin, finally. I seem like a New Yorker to them: exotic, ridiculous, impractical, and yet somehow credible (it must be the two books), or, if not entirely credible, at least worthy of trust. And I think they enjoy teaching me things, the roles reversed.

Writing classes are about trust, of course, and after a while, in the safe place we have created together they begin writing their dreams, their fantasies, their desires. What many of them write about again and again is a thing they have never seen— the ocean. I am so moved by their longing—these children of the Midwest, these children of ISU—cinder-blocked, land-locked. They swim in high water. They never tire. They begin to learn how to write themselves free.

My graduate class at first makes me a little nervous. After all, I have never been to graduate school myself. I have never been in a writing workshop before. I have never taught anyone anything. But they, too, are unreasonably kind.

Still, something is a little off. I am often lost there, disoriented. The boys seem too perfect, too polite. I am amazed at the heightened, garish sexual fantasies they inspire. And the girls—they're too complacent, too nice. I realize that part of why I'm here is to teach them to be bad, to question, to disobey. Normal: I feel on the edges of town and then out into the countryside, the severity of farmers, rising at dawn, eating dinner at five and to bed. They would not approve of me, these men. There's a certain unreality to everything I see or perceive. Here, where people still eat lots of beef and lots of candy bars and smoke cigarettes, and many—it is true, as the French like to say of Americans—are overweight. The fat people for the circus must be grown out here, I think in a dream. And even the university is a paradox, a very unusual place. On the outside it is a lot of ugly buildings plunked down in the middle of nowhere. On the inside there is a gleaming altar to the most innovative and experimental literature in the world. It is taught here, it is valued, it is even published. Illinois State now houses both Dalkey Archive Press and *The Review of Contemporary Fiction,* as well as Fiction Collective Two. And in the Unit for Contemporary Literature, the dream of a literary avant-garde utopia is slowly being realized. In this whole wide country there is no other place that comes close to it. Few places in the world come to mind. And my New York is light years away.

This land of stark miracle springing from the extraordinarily fertile earth. Flat earth. Where each night on the flatlands I dream of a curvaceous woman. She cups water in her hands. And I marvel at the beauty of the cornfields and the sky. Count pheasants. Visit what I've dubbed the Beckett tree, straight out of *Godot.* The land is breathtaking in its austerity, in its uncompromising forever, as gorgeous as anything I've ever seen. A different sort of ocean.

But I fear at times the cornfields and the miles and miles of soybean fields and the sky. We are up to our thighs in corn. We imagine we drink utterly pure, sweet water. Heartland water. Perfect water. But three younger women now, natives of this place, all from the heart of the heart of the country, are stricken with cancer, and I am forced to wonder what it is about. The pesticides in the sweet water? The beloved injected cows, that delicious, coveted beef? The feed?

This pristine countryside. We drive. I take my class hours and hours away to another school to see the great filmmaker Stan Brackhage, who has turned up to speak and show films. We are examining alternative narrative strategies in my graduate class. Hearing him speak and watching his extraordinary films in the dark, I forget for a few hours how far away I am from home. For a little while I am more at home than I am anywhere else.

I was expecting nothing. Then, after a while I was expecting an extreme provinciality from my central Illinois. But finally I have come to realize that it is no more provincial than one of the minor cities: Pittsburgh or Milwaukee, say. And, in fact, it may be somewhat better, who knows? I joined the Normal ACT UP, a branch that included maybe ten people. One freezing October night we read the names of those who had died all the way through until dawn, and there was a legion of people here to grieve all ages, all types. All night.

And of Chicago, I recognize immediately that it is a city I might, given the chance, come to love. I find myself more comfortable there than in any other American city I know outside of New York. It seems real—its architecture, its grandeur, its people, its cultural life, its miseries. I find it a relief after the pretty toy of San Francisco, the segregated contrivances of Boston, artificial D.C., sprawling, incomprehensible L.A. And the other cities: Houston, Atlanta, whatever. Who knew?

And in retrospect ISU will be among the best institutions I shall teach in. Schools that now include Columbia, Bennington, Brown.

And it is the first time I will ever be called a goddess. And it is the first time in my adult life that I will be able to pay my bills. Or go to the doctor.

The goddess is waiting again, having gone home to New York and having flown back to Chicago, for her all-too-small, all-too-private plane to take her back to Bloomington. I look for the dark angel I see each time in the propeller's rotating blade. So many hair-raising American Eagle trips that year, flights I was pretty sure I'd never get off alive. They were always cartoonish, it seemed, with drinks flying and ladies crying. Before boarding they would check our weight and the weight of our carry-ons, in order to assign seats. So much waiting that year. The wings are frozen solid again. I entertain the grim possibility that perhaps at last this will be my final flight.

There are many strange dangers. I have always feared the Midwest, I realize that now—known for its clean-cut serial killers, its smoldering, unreadable violences. When I walk into my friendly, neighborhood liquor store I literally see red before my eyes. Sometimes it's only for an instant, but sometimes it's something more prolonged. It's odd because I do not ordinarily have such visions, and yet the color is undeniable—red. Only much later do I learn of the triple murder that occurred there a year or so before. OK, maybe I, too, have come to die. I can't help wondering.

Or maybe I've come here just to dance: We pile into the truck in our glitter and bows and head for Peoria to the local gay club to watch our friend perform in drag. I am a little smug. I am of course from New York City, and dubious to say the least. In my time I have witnessed more than one cross-dressers' convention in Provincetown, that gay mecca, and I fancy myself something of an expert.

Peoria, Illinois. The audience in this grungy club is the weirdest mix: lots of working people, farmers and the like, their wives, businessman types, young lesbians, and gay men of all ages. I have never seen such a sight. Our friend appears center stage. It is *he* who is the goddess, with those cat eyes, those cheekbones, that perfect jaw, that smile. His hair is fabulous, his makeup is fabulous, his dress. He, or rather, she, is more amazing than anything I've seen, and she's just my type, too: a young, kind of decadent Bianca Jagger. She bends her knees, blows kisses, does a little turn. And the music begins. I wonder what the French would think. Nothing here is ever quite what it seems. And I must admit I am a little bit in love.

Precious, Disappearing Things

AVA IS A LIVING TEXT. One that trembles and shudders. One that yearns. It is filled with ephemeral thoughts, incomplete gestures, revisions, recurrences, and repetitions—precious, disappearing things. My most spacious form thus far, it allows in the most joy, the most desire, the most regret. Embraces the most uncertainty. It has given me the freedom to pose difficult questions and has taught me how to love the questions: the enduring mystery that is music, the pull and drag of the tide, the mystery of why we are here and must die.

No other book eludes me like *AVA*. It reaches for things just outside the grasp of my mind, my body, the grasp of my imagination. It brings me up close to the limits of my own comprehension, pointing out, as Kafka says, the incompleteness of any life—not because it is too short, but because it is a human life. *AVA* is a work in progress and will always be a work in progress. It is a book in a perpetual state of becoming. It cannot be stabilized or fixed. It can never be finished. It's a book that could be written forever, added to or subtracted from in a kind of Borgesian infinity. Do I ever finish putting things in order? Can I assign a beginning to affection, or an end? Every love affair returns, at odd moments, as a refrain, a handful of words, a thrumming at the temple perhaps, or a small ache at the back of the knee. *AVA* is filled with late last-minute things—postscripts, post-postscripts.

I come back to writing continually humbled and astonished. I do not pretend to understand how disparate sentences and sentence fragments that allow in a large field of voices and subjects, linked to each other quite often by mismatched syntax and surrounded by space for 265 pages, can yield new sorts of meanings and wholeness. I do not completely understand how such fragile, tenuous, mortal connections can suggest a kind of forever. How one thousand Chinese murdered in a square turn into one thousand love letters in the dying Ava Klein's abstracting mind, or how the delicate, coveted butterflies Nabokov chases on the hills of Telluride become a hovering and beautiful alphabet. I cannot really speak of these things. As Michael Palmer said of one of his volumes of poetry, "the mystery remains in the book." I can only discuss the writing of *AVA*.

I was promoting my novel *The Art Lover*. I was flying places, meeting people, connections were constantly being made and broken. I felt strange and estranged the way I do during such times, with all the reading, all the talking into black microphones, all the usual replies to the same questions over and over. Because I must write every day, I continued to write then, though I could only manage one or two sentences at a time. The next entry, some time later, would be another sentence, often unrelated to the one that had come before. I was using language as an anchor and a consolation, enjoying the act of simply putting one word next to another and allowing them to vibrate together. Most days it was my only pleasure. Shortly after the book promotion, North Point Press, scheduled to do my next book, *The American Woman in the Chinese Hat,* and also *The Art Lover* in paperback, folded. These books made the rounds at commercial houses where so-called literary editors displayed the usual ignorance and lack of vision I have now become more accustomed to, with their love of safety and product and money. But I was still capable of being shocked by them then. I kept writing in pieces. I was scheduled to escape to France and had sublet my apartment when a death prevented me from leaving the country. The fragments piled up. Keeping the notebooks going, I began to travel the world in my own way. Among the many voices I had accumulated I began to hear a recurring voice, an intelligence if you will. She was a thirty-nine-year-old woman, confined to a hospital bed and dying, yet extraordinarily free.

I cannot say what direction her story would have taken had it not been assuming its final form during the terrible weeks of the Persian Gulf war. It was my first war as an adult, and like everyone I watched the whole, awful thing live on TV. War as a subject permeates the text of *AVA,* but more importantly war dictates the novel's shape. A very deep longing for peace, one I must admit I had scarcely been aware of, overwhelmed me as I watched the efficient, precise elimination of people, places, things by my government. My loathing for the men who were making this, and my distrust of the inherited, patriarchal forms led me to search for more feminine shapes—less "logical" perhaps, since a terrible logic had brought us here—less simplistic, a form that might be capable of imagining peace, accommodating freedom, acting out reunion. I was looking for the fabric of reconciliation. Something that might join us. I was determined not to speak in destructive or borrowed forms any longer. But what did that mean? I began to ask the question of myself, "What could she not ask of fiction and therefore never get?" I began one more time to ask what fiction might be, what it might do, and what we might deserve, after all. Traditional fiction had failed us. Did we dare presume to dream it over? To discard the things we were given but were never really ours?

In an attempt to ward off death with its chaos and mess, traditional fiction had flourished. Its attempts to organize, make manageable and comprehensible with its reassuring logic, in effect, reassures no one. I do not think I am overstating it when I say that mainstream fiction has *become* death with its complacent, unequivocal truths, its reductive assignment of meaning, its manipulations, its predictability and stasis. As I was watching the war it became increasingly clear to me that this fiction had become a kind of totalitarianism, with its tyrannical plot lines, its linear chronology, and characterizations that left no place in the text for the reader, no space in which to think one's thoughts, no place to live. All the reader's freedoms in effect are usurped.

In an ordinary narrative I hardly have time to say how beautiful you are or that I have missed you or that—come quickly, there are finches at the feeder! In a traditional narrative there is hardly any time to hear the lovely offhand things you say in letters or at the beach or at the moment of desire. In *AVA* I have tried to write lines the reader (and the writer) might meditate on, recombine, rewrite as he or she pleases. I have tried to create a place to breathe sweet air, a place to dream. In an ordinary narrative I barely have the courage or the chance to ask why we could not make it work, despite love, despite everything we had going. In an ordinary narrative I would have probably missed the wings on Primo Levi's back as he stands at the top of the staircase. And Beckett too, during the war, hiding in a tree and listening to a song a woman sings across the sadness that is Europe.

"The ideal or the dream would be to come up with a language that heals as much as it separates." When I read this line by Hélène Cixous, I knew she was articulating what I was wordlessly searching for when I began to combine my fragments. "Could one," Cixous asks, "imagine a language sufficiently transparent, sufficiently supple, intense, faithful, so that there would be reparation and not only separation?" And yes, isn't it possible that language instead of limiting possibility might actually enlarge it? That through its suggestiveness, the gorgeousness of its surface, its resonant, unexplored depths, it might actually open up the world a little, and possibly something within ourselves as well? I agree with Barthes when he says that the novel and the theater (and not these essays by the way) are the natural settings in which concrete freedom can most violently and effectively be acted out. That this is not the case for the most part, in fiction at any rate, is a whole other matter relating back to the "literary" editors who have entered a covert, never-discussed, and possibly not even conscious conspiracy to conserve a certain aesthetic. Women, blacks, Latinos, Asians, etc., are all made to sound essentially the same—that is, say, like John Cheever, on a bad day. Oh, a few bones are thrown now and then, a few concessions are made to exotic or alternative or "transgressive" content, but that is all. And more freedom slips away.

All experience, of course, is filtered through one's personality, disposition, upbringing, culture (which is why I know we do not all sound like John Cheever). Truth be told I was never much for ordinary narrative, it seems. Even as a child, the eldest of five, I would wander year after year in and out of our bedtime reading room, dissatisfied by the stories, the silly plot contrivances, the reduction of an awesome complicated world into a rather silly, sterile one. When my mother was reading stories I would often wander out to the night garden, taking one sentence or one scene out there with me to dream over, stopping, I guess, the incessant march of the plot forward to the inevitable climax. Only when it came time for poetry did I sit transfixed. These seemed to me much closer an approximation of my world, which was all strangeness and wonder and light.

Back then my remote father grew roses. The tenderness of this fact, and the odd feeling I had that he cared more for these silent, beautiful creatures than he did for us, always intrigued and oddly touched me. It was what my childhood was: random, incomprehensible, astounding events, one after the next. I cherish this image of my father. And because I have never wholly understood it I gave Ava's father the task of growing roses. Unlike my father, Ava's father survived Treblinka. He gives Ava a penny apiece for each Japanese beetle she can collect from the garden. The Germans sold the dead Jews' hair for fifteen pennies a kilo. There were piles of women's hair there. Fifty feet high. Ava in her innocence and purity, holding her clear jar of beetles, says, "Yes, we'll have to make holes for the air." The book is built on waves of association like this. There is a rose called "Peace." A rose called "Cuisse de Nymphe Emue"—that's "Thigh of an Aroused Nymph." It blooms once unreservedly and then not again.

I have attempted in some small way to create a text, as Barthes says, "in which is braided, woven in the most personal way, the relations of every kind of bliss: those of 'life' and those of the text, in which reading and the risks of life are subjects to the same anamnesis."

Back to my mother reading me stories those long ago nights. Another thing I did was to detach the meanings from the words and turn them into a kind of music, a song my mother was singing in a secret language just to me. It was a rhythmic, sensual experience as she sang what I imagine were the syllables of pure love. This is what literature became for me: music, love, and the body. I cannot keep the body out of my writing; it enters the language, transforms the page, imposes its own intelligence. If I have succeeded at all you will hear me breathing. You will hear the sound my longing makes. You will sense in the text the body near water, as it was then, and in silence. Not the body as it is now, in Washington, D.C., next to obelisks and pillars and domes, walking it seems in endless circles and reciting the alphabet of those streets over and over. That will show up later; the body has an incredible memory.

My hope is that you might feel one moment of true freedom in *AVA*. That the form, odd as it may at first seem, will not constrict or alienate, but will set something in motion. Here I am always just on the verge of understanding, which is the true

state of desire. Perhaps you will feel some of this enormous
desire for everything in the world in the fragments of this living, changing, flawed work. And in the silence between fragments.

"Almost everything is yet to be written by women," Ava
Klein says, moments before her death.

Let us bloom then, unreservedly.

There's still time.

A Novel of Thank You

for Gertrude Stein

*B*EGIN in singing.

Chapter One
Rose.

A Longer Chapter
A word whispered. Called through green. In the years she was
growing and lilting hills sung in the night and in the day and
in every possible way over water rose the first word, the world.
Was I loving you I was loving you even then.

One word. Rose

To Be Sung
Urgently, sweetly, with bliss, and sometimes with desperation

Chapter Bliss
Rose.

Chapter Wish
Rose. And Chapter hope…

And this is what bliss is this.

Rose to be sung against the sky and diamonds night.

Red Roses
A cool red rose and pink cut pink, a collapse and a solid hole,
a little less hot

In direct sensuous relationship to the world.

Chapter Early and Late Please
I found myself plunged into a vortex of words, burning words,
cleansing words, liberating words, and the words were ours
and it was enough that we held them in our hands.

Chapter
Sincerely Beverly Nichols Avery Hopwood Allan Michaels
and Renee Felicity also how many apricots are there to a
pound.

And this is what bliss this is bliss this is bliss.

They found themselves happier than anyone who was alive
then.

Chapter Saint
Saint Two and Saint Ten
Saint Tribute
Saint Struggle

Chapter Grace
Chapter Faith
Chapter Example
Saint Admiration

Our Lady of Derision

Saint Deadline—not finished and not finishable. I like thinking of this.

How many saints are there in it? Saints we have seen so far:
Tributes are there in it? A Very Valentine—for Gertrude
Stein.
Colors are there in it?
A Novel of Thank You. A Basket.

Saint Example and Saint Admiration
Thank you, how many, audacity religiosity beauty and purity
your ease your inability to compromise ever thank you

very much.

Your freedoms Saint Derision, Chapter One
Do prepare to say
Portraits and Prayers, do prepare
to say that you have
prepared portraits and prayers and
that you prepare and that I prepare
    Yes you do.

A vortex of words very much.

For your irreverence and desire
extremity courage and good humorous

subversiveness
splendorous
    Yes you do.

For Your Beauteous
Language is a rose, a woman, constantly in the process of
opening
thank you

your freedoms. Released at last from the prisons of syntax.
Story.

For your—
Choose wonder.

Choose Wonder
Apples and figs burn.
They burn.

She had wished windows and she had wished.

A novel of thank you and not about it chapter one.

Rose, rose, rose.

Rose whispered, prayed over the child love love. Please please
sweet sweet sweet

Chapter
Susie Asado
Sweet sweet sweet sweet sweet tea
written for a particularly irresistible flamenco dancer

Please be please be get, please get wet, wet naturally, naturally
in weather.

Chapter Alice

To not emerge already constructed, already decided, preor-
dained.
Thank you

The difference is spreading.

very much

The permission.

I like the feeling of words doing as they want to do and as they
have to do

I like the feeling.

very much

The main intention of the novel was to say thank you.

A novel of thank you. In chapters and saints.

And it is easily understood that they have permission.

Without telling what happened...to make the play the essence
of what happened.

A thing you all know is that in the three novels written in this
generation that are important things written in this generation,
there is, in none of them a story. There is none in Proust in *The
Making of Americans* or in *Ulysses*.

Once upon a time they came every day and did we miss them
we did. And did they once upon a time did they come every
day. Once upon a time they did not come every day they never
had they never did they did not come every day any day.

A novel of thank you and not about it.

A story of arrangements

When it is repeated or Bernadine's revenge. When it is
repeated is another subject. How it is repeated is another
subject. If it is repeated is another subject. If it is repeated
or the revenge of Bernadine is another subject.

inner thought, silent fancies

There is one thing that is certain, and nobody realized it in the
1914–19 war, they talked about it but they did not realize it
but now everybody knows it everybody that the one thing that
everybody wants is to be free, to talk to eat to drink to walk to
think, to please, to wish, and to do it now if now is what they
want, and everybody knows it they know it anybody knows
it…1943

…not to be managed, threatened, directed, restrained, obliged,
fearful, administered

multiplicity and freedom unfettered ecstatic

thank you

To begin to allow. To allow it.

I had to recapture the value of the individual word, find out
what it meant and act within it.

Imagine a door.

To free oneself from convention again and again and again.
Thank you for suggesting once again. And again and again
that story is elsewhere, that story must have been, been else-

where. In every kind of other place. Thank you. Again and again. In every possible way.

Once upon a time they came every day and did we miss them we did. And did they once upon a time did they come every day. Once upon a time they did not come every day...

Chapters in the middle
So then out loud.
Everyone.
And so forth.
All and one and so forth.
By and one and so forth.

Grammar will. Grammar. Obliged.

Grammar is not grown.

Grammar means that it has to be prepared and cooked. Forget about grammar and think about potatoes.

Or gnocchi. We are touring Italy. Tuscany and Umbria a little.

Cypress cypress cypress cypress cypress pine.

Grammar is not grown.

Susan Howe, *My Emily Dickinson:* To restore the original clarity of each word-skeleton both women [Gertrude Stein and Emily Dickinson] lifted the load of European literary custom. Adopting old strategies, they revived and reinvented them...
Emily Dickinson and Gertrude Stein also conducted a skillful and ironic investigation of patriarchal authority over literary history. Who polices questions of grammar, parts of speech,

connection and connotation? Whose order is shut inside the structure of their sentence? What inner articulation releases the coils and complications of Saying's assertion? In very different ways the counter-movement of these two women's work penetrates to the indefinite limits of written communication.

No one can know the difference between why I did and why I did not.

Not that kind of novel then.

And in my own very gradual real move toward a more abstract fiction who have been the models? Woolf, Woolf, Beckett, Beckett, Woolf, Woolf, Woolf, then Stein, Stein, now Stein. Stein now for some time very much. I've been loving you following you Chapter Gratitude. Yes for some time, time now so what about it say for example John Reed?

John Reed: She (Stein) lives and dies alone, a unique example of a strange art.

And where have you gotten your chronology from for your master narratives? And what has it cost you?

And what have you taken for legibility? And what has it cost finally?

Be nice. Try to be.

Thank you for the strangeness and the beauty. Reality is remote say it.

Imagine a door a room plenty of ice and snow also as often as they came in they went out.
And so forth...

They finally did not continue to interest themselves in description.

Chapter Derision just the other day one of The Famous Postmodern Novelists says when asked about The Great American Writers: Oh not Gertrude Stein, no, no not Stein.

Joyce

Picasso on Joyce: He is an obscure writer all the world can understand.

Stein drains the text of psychological and mythical overtones thank you very much. She cannot be solved and thank you.

Leave me leave something to confusion.
And I thank you.
The central theme of the novel is that they were glad to see each other.

Susan Howe: In the college library I use there are two writers whose work refuses to conform to the Anglo-American literary traditions these institutions perpetuate. Emily Dickinson and Gertrude Stein are clearly among the most innovative precursors of modernist poetry and prose, yet to this day canonical criticism from Harold Bloom to Hugh Kenner persists in dropping their names and ignoring their work. Why these two pathfinders were women, why American—are questions too often lost in the penchant for biographical detail that "lovingly" muffles their voices.

A novel of thank you and not about it.

It is a much more impressive thing to anyone to anyone standing, that is not in action than acting or doing anything doing anything being a successive thing but being something existing. That is then the difference between narrative as it has been and narrative as it is now. And this has come to be a natural thing in a perfectly natural way that the narrative of today is not a narrative of succession as all writing for a good many hundreds of years has been.

A space of time filled with moving.

To want everything at once. To write everything at once.

Susan Howe: Writing was the world of each woman. In a world of exaltation of *his* imagination, feminine inscription seems single and sudden.

Chapter Alice, Chapter Jane, Chapter Karen, Chapter Gina.

Chapters in the middle
Notes to myself: The plays conceived as painting. To be apprehended all at once. Meditations inviting dreaming, dalliance. Yet filled with internal movement. Living in itself. Intensity and calm. Mystery and joy. Surprise, delight. Robert Wilson's *Four Saints* last summer. Bliss. Joyous. Well fish.

A novel is a continual surprise.

Chapters as literary device rather than the natural division of novelistic time.

Listening to the Baltimore aunts telling the same stories over and over but each time a little differently.

Ricotta with a pear. This is a story of that in part. Don't forget the pecorino. In part.

A novel of thank you in chapters and saints. Children and fish.
Thank you for desire. Reverence and Irreverence. Repeating.

Saints I have definitely seen so far.
Saint Catherine
Saint Francis
Saint Clare definitely

I am calling from Italy to say that there is smoke coming out of
my computer and she says is there still a picture when you use
the battery and I say yes and she says don't worry it will all be
OK wait until I get there. And I tell her I will meet her in the
fortezza and I do, and it is.

The central theme of the novel is that they were glad to see
each other.

A very valentine.

An arrangement of their being there and never having been
more glad than before…

I will wait for you in the fortezza for as long as it takes.

Chapter written in the very hot sun while waiting.
Seeing Saint Catherine's Head. (Siena)

Loving repeating is one way of being. This is now a description
of such being. Loving repeating is always in children. Loving
repeating is in a way earth feeling. Some children have loving
repeating for little things and storytelling, some have it as a
more bottom being. Slowly this comes out in them in all their
children being, in their eating, playing, crying and laughing.
Loving repeating is then in a way earth feeling. This is very
strong in many, in children and in old age being. This is very

strong in many in all ways of humorous being, this is very strong in some from their beginning to their ending.

Chapter Emily Rose and Katie Grosvenor

Again and again and again

A very valentine

How are the cats?

Thank you

Go red go red, laugh white.
Suppose a collapse in rubbed purr, in rubbed purr get.
Little sales ladies little sales ladies
Little saddles of mutton.
Little sales of leather and such
beautiful beautiful, beautiful beautiful.

Most tender buttons.

Trembling was all living, living was all loving, someone was then the other one.

Please may I have a piece of your Pecorino di Pienza thank you very much.

We have been planning a little trip to Italy in June.

Any time is the time to make a poem. The snow and sun below.

A short novel in cats
She loved her little black and white.
She loved her orange very much.
She loved her gray.

She loved her brown stripes.
But she loved her gray the most. Fauve.

It is because of this element of civilization that Paris has
always been the home of all foreign artists, they are friendly
the French, they surround you with a civilized atmosphere
and they leave you inside of you completely to yourself.

An inner language

Merci beaucoup.

How many more than two are there. (I miss gossiping with you)

And I was once or twice in Vence and loving you very much.
Chapter J and Z.

And on the rue de Fleurus.

The Germans were getting nearer and nearer Paris and the
last day Gertrude Stein could not leave her room, she sat and
mourned. She loved Paris, she thought neither of manuscripts
nor of pictures, she thought only of Paris and she was desolate.
I came up to her room, I called out, it is all right Paris is saved,
the Germans are in retreat. She turned away and said, don't
tell me these things. But it's true, I said, it is true. And then
we wept together.

And then we wept.

How muffled the world suddenly—as if walking through
snow

to the last village of Zenka, perched on a hill

where forever resides, and hasn't it been nice?

Having gone to London in the month of May and roses to say good-bye.

Already I miss you very much.

Chapter 5
And how to thank you.
It was very nearly carefully in plenty of time.

Could if a light gray and heart rending be softer could it and light gray be paler could it and light gray be paler. Not the least resemblance between that and that.

Once more. Thank you very much. Once more. Once. Twice. Once more. I shall miss you. The things we used to do and say. And how we will not get to the Lago Giacomo Puccini this time.

The patience of a saint.
Not this time.

It takes a lot of time to be a genius, you have to sit around so much doing nothing, really doing nothing. If a bird or birds fly into the room is it good luck or bad luck we will say it is good luck.

A novel of thank you and a travel diary. With and without birds. Looking for an Agritourismo late at night. How many saints have we seen so far?

Saint Francis definitely all over the place, and Saint Clare and Saint Catherine from before.

And how many parts of saints?

Pray to the rib of the saint for strength. The leg of the saint.

It was not a mistake.

Allowed to watch composition. Witness creation. Thank you thank you.

Written in Venice on "honeymoon": A sonatina. Pussy said that I should wake her in an hour and a half if it didn't rain. It is still raining what should I do.

Secrets, gossips, hopes, disappointments, household life, erotic life, artistic doubts, apologies, jokes, intimacies.

And if not the real story, then what the story was for me.
Chapter Ava.
Don't leave anything out.
To accomplish wishes one needs one's lover.
—for Helen P

Can we stay in Pienza one more day?

Don't leave anything out.

This must not be put in a book.
Why not.
Because it mustn't.
Yes sir.

Chapter
I know at least four or five Amys now.

To begin to allow. To allow it.

She was not to come again. She came and she asked and she was answered and she was not to come again not to come she was asked and she was answered and she was answered and she was asked and she was not to come again well she was not to come again. This is the first time she came she was not to come again. To reason with Bertha and Josephine and Sarah and Susan and Adela and never Anns. What is the difference between chocolate and brown and sugar and blue and cream and yellow and eggs and white. What is the difference between addition and edges and adding and baskets and needing and pleasure. It was not a mistake.

When she was and help me when she was what was she to me.

...generosity depends upon what is and what is not held out and held up and held in that way.

Allow flowers.

A basket—for Gertrude Stein. And for Alice add flowers. And some eggs.

Explain looking. Explain looking again. Alice
explain looking again.

The sound of thinking and the sound of thought. A piece of thinking. Don't forget to add flowers. First poppies and broom and then after awhile sunflowers come out. The yellow hovering.

Every color of saint.
Blue saints green saints yellow saints black saints and red angels.

A back and forth. A basket.

We need transference of letters and parcels and doubts and dates and easier.
A novel is useful in more ways than one.

Someday we will be rich. You'll see and then we will spend money and buy everything a dog a Ford letter paper, furs, a hat, kinds of purse.

For Helen, touring Italy. And we will buy a villa someday or a farm if that is what you really want I love you. A Florentine chandelier and a Venetian one. Two more Maine coons perhaps (another gray, another one with stripes) and time to write and all the time in the world to write. Maybe another orange one.

What would you buy?
I would buy all the time in the world to write. I'd quit my job. Because it takes all the time.

One wish: 1) time to write.
              2) time to write.
And after that.
              time to write.

Stretches and stretches of happiness.

More time.

Left.
Left.
Pretty.
I
had
pretty
a
good
pretty.

I often think about another.

Who need never be mentioned.

Lifting belly high.
That is what I adore always more and more.

Some Amys in that way and some not.

A basket and so forth and what got lost.

Delirious and looking up from lip and clitoris and mound she sees the city of Paris lit up. Trembling was all living, living was all loving, someone was then the other one. The women walk the streets syntactic. Sing Paris Paris Paris Paris. A large white poodle dog and walking down the boulevard.

Chapter Pussycat
Touring through that part of Italy. Her meals: written in a notebook—penne with funghi, game hen with Norcia sauce, tiramisu.

She came to be happier than anyone else who was living then.

She came to be happier…In the gorgeous city of Paris. Poodle dog. Yellow flowered hat. Alice Babette.

10,000 paradises

Everyone dies. Say it enough times. Everyone dies everyone dies everyone even you everyone

with and without cats
with and without baskets

dies 10,000 kinds of thank you and paradise

First religion   She saw me and she said two
will stay and two will go away, two will go away and two
will stay and two will stay and two will go away. Can you go
away so soon.

First religion   First religion here.

Second religion   Second religion here.

Third religion   Third religion here.

Fourth religion   Fourth religion being here and having
her and she having been and she is perfection.

Third religion   Third religion being here or is she perfection third religion is here and she is perfection.

Third religion or is she perfection.

We have left the cathedral behind us. Saints seen so far:

How many saints are there in it?

Beginning again and again is a natural thing…Beginning
again and again and again explaining composition and time is
a natural thing

A Little Novel
Any and everyone is an authority.
Welcome.
Does it make any difference who comes first.

What Does She See When She Shuts her Eyes, a novel
So the characters in this novel are the ones who walk in the
fields and lose their dog and the ones who do not walk in the
fields because they have no cows.

When she shuts her eyes she sees the green things among
which she has been working and then as she falls asleep she
sees them a little differently.

When she shuts her eyes…Everyone dies. I can't cope. A gun
would be nice. What's wrong with me? Please say it soon.
Everyone dies.

You have cancer.
Why do you lie?

Everyone.

A Short Novel
I feel useless

Is it in any particular corner?

What does she see when she shuts her eyes a novel.

Paradise. What does she see?

And how to thank you.
You changed my life.
And how to thank you.
It was nearly very carefully in plenty of time.

This is the time to do or say so.
Chapter

Not useless. Not a bird. Not a cherry. Not a third. Not useless.
Not at all. Not elite. Not small.

It's useless.

So the characters in this novel are looking out the window of
a green Fiat touring Italy and one of them is thinking about
Gertrude Stein and reading her out loud in between cypress
cypress cypress and the map and the guidebook and I feel
useless.

Zenka.

The month of June and Defiance due and *The Bay of Angels*
excerpt due and The novel of thank you due for Martine. And
that perfectly awful woman Mattie Garrett at the Tuscany
Writing Workshop and the computer up in smoke.

Oh that perfectly awful Mattie Garrett, she thought turning
toward the dark window, has spoiled all of our fun!

The fax this afternoon. Useless.

Blue birds on a black hat. And as it happens. Black birds on a
blue hat. And as it happens. Blue birds on a blue hat. And not
next to as it happens. Black bird and a black hat.

Chapters 84 and almost 85, but not quite

People die in and out of order
in easy and hard ways people die
people die out of—
The things we used to do
sweetness of the yellow broom.
even though you are 84
even though everyone must
everyone has got to

in or out of order
drinking vieux marc, a trip to the sea
as if love could send you back there again
swept up, side swept, wind
like magic as if love
your beloved Dylan Thomas and Eliot your friend,
he was always kind, he lent me money, not anti-Semitic, he
lent me money, nonsense, oh such nonsense.
And your Gertrude Stein

People die in 5, 6, 7 and
7, 6, 5
in the day and the night.
Afraid and not.

Happy and sad times.
And that fall how I just thought if I could make a pot-au-feu
I might survive—and you looked on sadly. And you took my
hand after awhile. That fall you saved my life. For the first
time. Thank you.

And if I could only help you now. Somehow. I want to very
much.

Elissa and Annabelle and Anatole. Dale and Julie and Suzanne
and Marilyn and Monica and the French Carole
and Diana Chapmann she's called.

Judith.

Urgent. My darling Zenka passed away this morning. She was
in the nursing home. Please call. Love, Judith

Letting love to have a mother. Letting love to have letting love
to have a mother letting love to have.

In plenty of time.

Rose. The first word, the first world I know.
Thank you in every possible way.

Preparing a novel and paving the way.

Catherine, Caroline, Charlotte, and Celestine.
In the place of no one not yet.

Miss miss miss miss miss and gossip

When they cannot stop it altogether when they cannot stop it altogether.

Come and kiss me when you want to because if you do you have more than done that which is a satisfaction to have been most awfully obliged to have as a delight and more than that.

Thank you.

Very much very much and as much and as much and then markets, markets are open in the morning and except on Monday.

Do you think we should follow the sign for Perugia?

very much

Chapters of magic near the beginning and end (interchangeable)

Puccini is striped like the campanile but it's all right.

Sage grows.

Very content followed by five bells.
We are very well fish.

Sage grows so let it.
Children grow.
Let them.
Ideas.
Notions of the novel
So let them.

Wild capers grow everywhere.
A tribute to Gertrude Stein and a travel diary so let it.
Roses and rosemary everywhere

For my
beautiful mother
Rose
Marie
Maso
the one word
of my world my father calling across the green
Rose

Chapter Always
These days thinking of you, always, always.

Chapter Alice
who named her Rose in hope, as the century turned 31

Grandma Alice very much

If they say and it is an established fact if they say that he has gone away is there anybody to ask about it. It is so very easy to change a novel a novel can be a novel and it can be a story of the departure of Dr. Johnston it can be the story of the discovery of how after they went away nobody was as much rested as they hoped to be.

Everything that will be said will have a connection with paper and amethysts with writing and silver with buttons and books.

I am a simple girl in some ways do not want the Isle of Capri the Lago Giacomo Puccini will do. If not this time then next. Looking all over Florence for the cross that got lost.

Consider whether they would be at all interested.

It can be easily seen that a novel of elegance leaves something to be desired.

Repeat. It can be easily seen that a novel of elegance leaves something to be desired. She knew in about the middle of it. Time to write.

Let me say it here. Everything I loved or wanted or feared.

Accuse me if you like one more time of overreaching. I miss you. Love you. Want.

And time to write.

This spa water is only for drinking. And the woman makes a breaststroke through the air, for swimming Bagno Vignoni, 30 kilometers away let's go.

In the green Fiat. Have to finish Gertrude Stein, have to finish Traveling Light—and the hills and the cypresses. Cypress, cypress, cypress, pine. Ava Klein turn over on your side.

There is never any altogether the easiest way is to leave out anything.

The whole chapter is thinking about the courage you afford and thinking out loud and the flowers and so not to be afraid. There is music in the head so sing continuously.

Chapter Rose
Who named you Carole Alice at mid-century. Thank you in every possible way.

Song of joy

And say what you need and like and want. Pleasure. A novel and you out loud. When she has been satisfied when she has been satisfied.

Begin again.

She may be coming in any moment darling.

Begin again.
Fanny irresistible.
Jenny recalled.
Henrietta as much as that.
Claribel by and by
Rose as plainly seen
Hilda for that time
Ida as not famous.
Katherine as it should have it in preference
Caroline and by this time
Maria by this arrangement Esther who can be thought of
Charlotte and finally.

She rolls the rosy aureole and pearl the world around and round. Sea pearl to pearl with her and lip she shudders honey gold and conjures—this must be Paradise—or maybe Paris. She came to be happier than anybody else who was alive then. Gorgeous lilting rosy pearl. She rides the women world syntactic. Sings Paris Paris Paris Paris. And they walk the poodle Basket.

Thank you.
The way it looks exactly like it.

The way you can get it to look exactly like you see and feel. Almost exactly. Thank you most of all for that.

Who in this world is luckier than I?

A very valentine—for Gertrude Stein.

Little by little and more and more I begin to understand you very much.

A novel and the future of the novel and the rest and the rest is diamonds.

Father calling to Mother, Rose across the world first word. Repeated again and again rose rose rose rose rose rose rose.

A novel of thank you and not about it.
It might be allowed

With thanks to Nicole Cooley, Keith Waldrop, John O'Brien, Catherine Stimpson.

Someone named Rose at mid-century named her.
In hope. 5 joyful 5 sorrowful mysteries.
Thank you in every possible way

Once more I thank you.

An arrangement of their being there and never having been more glad than before.

A list of addresses and who went to see them.

Bruschetta, crostoni, lentils with pasta, grilled lamb, tiramisu.

Spaghetti with clam sauce.

Come and kiss me when you want to.

We are very well fish
Lavishly well fish

And Alice Babette, petite crevette. On the rue Christine after the war. Adore. Picking flowers gentle. Rose is a rose is a rose eternal and I am I because my little dog knows me.
She wanders gorgeous key syntactic. Violet-breasted. Poodle Basket.

Third religion	Where.
Fourth religion	Where they grow vegetables so plentifully.
Fourth religion	If you courtesy.
Second religion	If you hold a hat on your head.
Third religion	If they are not told.
Fourth religion	Across to me.
Fourth religion	She walked across to me.
Third religion	And what did she see.
Second religion	What did she say to me.
First religion	When she walked across to me.

I found myself plunged into a vortex of words, burning words, cleansing words, liberating words, and the words were all ours and it was enough that we held them in our hands...

I shall not speak for anybody. I shall do my duty, I shall establish that mile. I shall choose wonder. Be blest.

Footnotes

Our Walks
Often in the evening we would walk together; I greeted at the
door of 5 rue Christine by Gertrude's staunch presence, pleasant touch of hand, well-rounded voice always ready to chuckle.
Our talks and walks led us far from war paths. For generally
having no ax to grind nor anyone to execute with it, we felt
detached and free to wander in our own quarter where, while
exercising her poodle, Basket, we naturally fell into thought
and step. Basket, unleashed, ran ahead, a white blur, the ghost
of a dog in the moonlit side streets:

> Where ghosts and shadows mingle—
> As lovers, lost when single.

The night's enchantment made our conversation as light, iri-
descent and bouncing as soap bubbles, but as easily exploded
when touched upon—so I'll touch on none of them for you,
that a bubble may remain a bubble! And perhaps we never
said *d'imperissables choses.*—Nathalie Barney

Sweetnotes

Their Cakes
The discovery of cakes had always been a peacetime pursuit of
Gertrude and Alice. Meeting them by chance at Aix-le-Bains, I
enquired why they happened to be on the opposite bank of the
Lac du Bourget, and was informed of a new sort of cake created in one of the villages on a mountain beyond. But first
obliged to go on errands, they descended from the lofty seat of
their old Ford car—Alice bejeweled as an idol and Gertrude
with the air of an Indian divinity.

She accepted her fame as a tribute, long on the way but due, and enjoyed it thoroughly. Only once, in Paris—and indeed the last time I saw her—did the recognition of a cameraman displease her, for he waylaid her just as we were entering Rumpelmayer's patisserie. In order to satisfy the need for cake, and the photographer's wish, she was photographed by him, through the plate-glass window, eating the chosen one.

Her meals—continued
Melon and prosciutto, artichoke risotto, grilled sausages, another tiramisu. Ravioli with truffles, fish stew, panecotta, and so forth.

Please another Piero della Francesca.

And so forth
I am not striving at all but only gradually growing and becoming steadily more aware of the way things can be felt and known in words, and perhaps if I feel them and know them myself in the new ways it is enough, and if I know fully enough there will be a note of sureness and confidence that will make others know too. And when one has discovered and evolved a new form it is not the form but the fact that *you are the form* that is important.

I find you young writers worrying about losing your integrity and it is well you should, but a man who really loses his integrity does not know that it is gone, and nobody can wrest it from you if you really have it.

Hemingway you have a small income; you will not starve; you can work without worry and you can grow and keep this thing and it will grow with you. But he did not wish to grow that way, he wished to grow violently.

Everybody's life is full of stories; your life is full of stories; my life is full of stories. They are very occupying, but they are not very interesting. What is interesting is the way everyone tells their stories.

Thornton Wilder: The fundamental occupation of Miss Stein's life was not the work of art but the shaping of a theory of knowledge, a theory of time, and a theory of the passions... the formalization of a metaphysics.

Mina Loy: She swept the literary circus clear for future performances.

For a very long time everybody refuses and then almost without a pause almost everybody accepts. In the history of the refused in the arts and literature the rapidity of the change is always startling.

Wassily Kandinsky, 1910: The apt use of a word (in its poetical sense), its repetition, twice, three times, or even more frequently, according to the need of the poem, will not only tend to intensify the internal structure but also bring out unsuspected spiritual properties in the word itself. Further, frequent repetition of a word (a favorite game of children, forgotten in later life) deprives the word of its external reference. Similarly, the symbolic reference of a designated object tends to be forgotten and only the sound is retained. We hear the pure sound, unconsciously perhaps, in relation to the concrete or immaterial object. But in the latter case pure sound exercises a direct impression on the soul. The soul attains to an objectless vibration, even more complicated, I might say more transcendent, than the reverberations released by the sound of a bell, a stringed instrument or a fallen board. In this direction lie the great possibilities for literature of the future.

Martin Ryerson: If you realized that she worked insistently, every day, to be published the first time by a real publisher, publishing house after she was sixty. But I wonder who will do that, who will have the insistence, you understand the obsession, the surety the purity of insistence to do that. No concessions. She used to tell me, Don't you ever dare to make a concession. Then one walks down, down, down. There's no end of walking down.

Acts
Curtain
Characters
Characters
Curtain
Acts
There is no one and one
Nobody has met anyone.
      Curtain Can Come.
      (for Zenka Bartek 1912–1997)
      Curtain.

And this is
what bliss
is and
this and
this is
what
bliss is.

very much

White lights lead to red lights which indicate the exit.

Spaghetti arrabiata, spaghetti bolognese, polenta, grilled pork, escarole, spinach, ricotta, tiramisu...

Saint Francis hundreds of times, Saint Sebastian certainly, Saint Simon, Saint Clare is a big one, the head of Saint Catherine, Saint Francis is a very big one, Saint Peter and Saint John of course. Saint Bliss.

Preparing a novel prepared to stay.

And paving the way.

Thank you very much.

Chapter Rose
Even then I was loving you

very much.

End in singing.

Who goes away tonight. They all do. And so they do.

Richter, the Enigma

WHAT IS THE LIMIT OF SNOW?

*N*OT A NOTE OF MUSIC in his parent's house. An apprentice-ship in silence.

The Fourth Violin Concerto (1984) has a cadenza which is to be seriously mimed by the soloist without making a sound. A tribute to the house of his birth.

He wore those fingerless gloves even as a toddler, before he became anything like a musical prodigy.

He remains to this day (15 October 1999) almost totally un-known outside of musical circles.

The dissonant Soviet avant-garde persona he loved to put on at parties. Richter, born in that less-than-restless New Jersey suburb, Upper Montclair, to American parents and given the unlikely name: Gustave Richter.

Once in high school Richter and I sitting on the curb, happily singing Frank Zappa songs. *Call any Vegetable, Saint Alphonzo's Pancake Breakfast,* etc.

Celebrating Edgar Varèse Day. We were despised by the other students. Of course.

Of course we were.

Density 21.5 performed in its entirety.

Composed for his graduation from the Julliard School of Music: *Uncle Pehrs's Life in Music.* 1978.

Richter walking through snow and Schoenberg.

Richter walking through the kind of snow you just don't see anymore. Into music.

B A C H (B flat) The letters of Bach's name appearing as a motif in much of his work.

"History is plundered, irony is rampant, pastiche becomes the only coherence."

The critic says, "He takes the style that mocks the very idea of genius and turns it into an affirmation of genius."

He is a master of modern melancholy and sarcasm. Yes he is.

Irony is a temptation, never a solution.

"Everything which causes disharmony in the world, all that is monstrous, inexplicable, and dreadful is an intrinsic part of the world's order. Disharmony and cacophony, 'the world's evil,' is knit into what is harmonious and beautiful." Richter in an interview last year.

His last piece: *For the Two Million Armenian Martyrs.*

What Richter loved:
the limits of perpetual snow.

Uncle Pehrs.

What concerned him was music, purely music and nothing else, yet there he is adjusting the shutter.

Hello!

Jean Sibelius's Uncle Pehrs hanging above his desk to this day.

A birthday party in Spain, that sort of documentation: I, tipsy hope to find him in the frame, champagne. The neck cut off with a knife. Richter grinning.

No one is commissioning Richter for anything. Money is, as always, a problem. Richter's assistant is despondent, etc. We walk around Central Park. Richter doing a lot of shrugging.

"…the profound and the absurd…is the tangible personal struggle that appears embedded in each piece." That's my friend Richter all right.

Richter in motion—where are you going?

The little Super 8 I bought him as a gift. He aims it in every which direction. We both lament that we do not have the temperament to participate in what is indisputably the most important art form of the century. *You've got to admit…*

It doesn't stop him from trying…in his spare time. Because, as he likes to explain to me, composers have a lot of spare time.

Set up on a tripod. 25 reels of Richter exist.

Happy New Year!

The Age of Discovery. The urge to solve the problem of recreating life in motion was tremendous. The motion picture was truly a child of its time. It was one of many problems solved, concepts realized, and inventions perfected.

Music for film: the sound of one woman weeping. Accompanied by a shimmering chorus of boys.

Richter and I sit and ponder Antonioni's *Eclipse.* 58 shots that last 7 minutes each. Richter says we are going to play these numbers in the lottery and that we are going to be rich. And we will publish all my unpublishable novels as they are written and we will have all his work performed in the great concert halls for the first time anywhere in this order: 1) *Adventures in a Perambulator,* 2) *For Blanca and Ulrich Love on the Occasion of the Fall of the Berlin Wall,* 3) *For Irina Wherever You May Be,* 4) *Uncle Pehrs's Life in Music,* 5) *One Chance in a Million,* 6) *That Which Does Not Kill Me, Makes Me Stronger,* 7) *Tango For Endurance Dancers,* 8) *Themes Heard on the Evening of Good Friday: for the Two Million Armenian Martyrs,* 9) *The White Island,* 10) *etc.*

From *The White Island* notebook, the story of August Linder, attempting to sail around the world in a hot air balloon—an opera-in-progress:

 "*17 September: Sited land for the first time yet landing is out of the question—the whole island seems a block of ice.*"

Reel 7—Richter and his page turner. The score illuminated by a single lamp—all else is darkness.

"Dear Father, the balloon is now inflated. I feel as if…" Richter looks to the sky.

I scribble stanzas on the back of an airmail envelope. Waving to him.

His mother: *"This is the first grief you have brought me, August."*

What is the weight of a human life high above the earth in a hot air balloon?

Richter—his footprints in snow. His favorite way to compose.

"Uncannily he can change the character of the music from one moment to another. There is absolutely no gap—as if he had improvised on the spot."

B A C H—a light in the dark.

His lifelong idol Alfred Schnittke. *Another stroke,* Richter says glumly.

One middle of the night—*Is Frank Zappa really dead?* Richter he is as far as I know, still dead. In a manner of speaking of course. *Yes, yes,* he mutters and hangs up.

If there is one chance in a million (to be sung) *then it must be Alfred Schnittke's! If there is one chance …*

How he goes from one thing to the next without transition.

In Garni two million fruit trees planted for the two million Armenian martyrs. A sacred forest. Richter, makes a detour on the way to

Reel 17: The limits of snow, language, music, human sorrow. The newly fallen

motion and the waning century and Richter waving from the

perpetual eternal snow

There is too much sorrow. Richter in motion.

Richter in sound.

Awaiting to this day its American premiere.

Tango for Endurance Dancers—composed in the early 80s. An attempt on my part convince the Ramapo High School Reunion Committee into a kind of Richter marathon. Received this afternoon a one-sentence response: "You have *got* to be kidding."

Collected Songs Where Every Verse is Filled with Grief.

I see him still climbing up, up into that mountain with his metal box of 26 reels, into the music.

Triads, he said calmly when asked over cocktails what—*triads, at the top of their register.*

Meditations at 33,000 feet. Richter old and grizzled far beyond his years, slumped in his black coat looks out the window and marvels.

The Age of Discovery. By five months many babies have both the head-up and bottom-up position perfected but cannot put the two together so as to be on hands and knees. They therefore alternate the two, and look as if they were see-sawing— first one end up and the other down and then the other up. By this stage a true crawl with the tummy clear of the floor is very unusual though quite a lot of babies will make some progress across the floor as they see-saw.

Reels 10–26: Richter in motion. That scarf blowing around his head.

Come on baby, do the locomotion, he sang once to me from Basel. Was it Basel? And then began to weep.

He was my best friend, but I barely knew him.

Richter on tiptoe: *I ask you, what is the limit of snow?*

The weight of 26 reels of film is surprisingly light. They disappeared with Richter. I can hardly bear to think about it.

Yes, the evidence. The proof that you are, or are not.

I will marry a woman named Irina, he said on one of those 26 reels.

I will have children and write them music and never, never leave the house again.

In my head this well-behaved fictive Richter. Reclusive, OK, but safe. Safe, at any rate.

I once heard someone found a frame of reel 17 preserved in snow in which it appears my friend, he is waving, the arm lifted, a sustained ascending scale, an instant of pure Richter. A perfect instant of Richter, lost, then found, then lost again.

A little bit of Richter is sent back. Lifting that little bit of Richter, I wonder, what is the weight of a human life?

Sprinkled around the potted plant. The hum of him. The little bit of Richter left.

Who Richter was.

Photography is born: the permanent recording of reality. So they say. So they say.

What can be known.

What can be loved (a part of speech, a diminished seventh, the way the ocean…the eye flickering as the day opens and the world begins again) but never known.

A star glide, the elision of lives, an instant in time, there: preserved by the yearbook photographer: Richter and I singing on a curb, least likely to succeed, most despised. *Let's make the water turn black.* Heard over the freeze frame.

The moment. Eluding the many possible ways to memorialize it.

I might call this little ditty "Richter, the Enigma." Because calling is what we seem to like to do. There is silliness to us.

He took with him the 26 reels. The evidence, we might say.

Richter in reel 3 stumbling toward the lens in silence. Not quite silence. From the back of the room, the projector's whir.

Reel 3:
Richter, swimming. Doing a bit of underwater photography. Singing at below sea-level.

Reel 4:
Ice fishing.

Reel 24:
Richter and Irina and baby Alfred…

Oh why tonight all these fictive Richters mixing up the so-called real one? What is the point? What is the use?

This figment of Richter. The moon, a sliver.

(ev' i d ns) n. 1. ground for belief; that which lends to prove or disprove something; proof. 2. something that makes evident;

an indication or sign. 3. *Law.* data presented in a court or jury of the facts which may include...

4. **in evidence**, plainly visible, conspicuous: *the first signs of spring are in evidence.*

I barely knew him. He aims his little Polaroid at the still obscured

intent on photographing Mount Ararat, and other impossible projects. A photographic essay provisionally titled: *Faith.*

From the blur after 99 days, emerges the subject.

He goes back to work.

He was my friend, Richter, but now he is gone. His footprints in the snow. The first signs of spring are in evidence. All that's left is the sound.

for G.R. 1955–1999
and for R.V.

Except Joy

on *Aureole*

Aureole CELEBRATES THE RESPLENDENCE of language and desire. It is a work of reverie and ruin. Pleasure. Oblivion. Joy. A place where we are for a little while endlessly possible, capable of anything, it seems: fluid, changing, ephemeral, renewable, intensely alive, close to death, clairvoyant, fearless, luminous, passionate, strange even to ourselves.

It was written in a kind of waking dream, an erotic hallucination in which I was only semiconscious and yet utterly lucid. I abandoned myself to the pressure, the touch of language, its sexual slur, the trance of it. The motions of the alphabet. I have tried to be attentive to its needs—its positions and shifts, its murmurings. The word's attraction for the word.

I write this now in Paris, city of light, in sweet breeze, in first heat, *golden square devour me*—after a winter so vast and white. *Aureole* was composed in a blizzard of emotion, in a blur of want, in an audacity of trust. I was knowing and unknowing, conscious and unconscious, freezing and fevered. Passion pressing these pieces into shapes like the press of animal tracks in the snow. The heat of the living body. The hope was for a language as ancient as memory, as direct as a moan, as gorgeous as song, as imperfect as utterance. It is in love with beauty and abandon and excess, unapologetically. The desire all winter was for transformation, transcendence. Now when I lift my dreaming head all of a sudden spring has come, *golden square,* and it is Paris; I marvel as the Seine turns into the Ganges, or the Hudson River, glistening, flowing through us on a white bed, on our pleasure river bed. The river being pulled through me like a miraculous, golden thread.

Aureole was shaped by desire's magical and subversive qualities. It imposed its swellings, its ruptures, its erasures, its motions. Sometimes wild, sometimes elusive, playful, wayward —it was driven by pleasure and forged in passion. I have tried to feel the sexual intoxication of the line or the page or the narrative—language overcome or desperate or greedy. The story staggered. The phrase gasping or begging or sighing.

With some dismay I realize that I am content in these pages to be, as Yeats said, "for the song's sake, a fool." I have overexposed myself in this work. I have gone too far and also not far enough, I have wandered off hoping to get close to that translucent, ephemeral thing. That impossible thing. Escaping. And the white page whispered back, continues to whisper back, *look, you're no match for it.*

Aureole resists categorization. My desire is far messier, more voracious, stranger than any existing or prescribed shape could accommodate. In fact I felt exiled, alien among those options. I could not recognize myself there. Desire pressing itself into odd shapes insistently, urgently, in a way I did not dare second-guess. The impulse in these pieces is to free myself from constraint, from preconception. The flight is from boundaries—linguistic, sexual, intellectual. The longing is for freedom.

Desire has made it possible for me to write into my greatest vulnerabilities, uncertainties. It has made it possible to not worry so much about the consequences, to let go a little. Desire has allowed me to write into its danger, its bliss, its silence, its abyss. To not care about failing. Whether these pieces were any "good" or not seemed hardly to enter it. I chose not to rely on facility. If I felt I was doing something I already knew how to do well, the rule was to start again in an attempt to break habitual patterns of mind and expression. I've tried to write into the heart of longing, regret, unsure once I was there how I would get back or if I'd get back. I have practiced courage a long time. I think of *The Art Lover*. Feigned it even when I did not have it, waiting for it to come. I've tried to write into reluctance—to actually feel the pull forward and back simultaneously, an erotic motion in itself. In this time of witness, of storytelling, I've tried to allow myself to walk into forgetfulness, dissolution. To give up a little. To let the earth go, and the ones I love most. To let a new logic take over. To live at the heart of the unknown, without explanation. Desire has allowed me to stray, to wander away from the familiar, to move far off into the landscape of passion or addiction—oblivion—snow or hope—the trance of our days here....

Language for me has always been a profoundly sensual experience. Language *is* emotion, language *is* feeling, language *is* body. It is not merely the sign for something, but rather also a thing in itself. It has weight and heat; it emits light. Its meaning is inseparable from its sound, its rhythms, the way it is arranged on the page. It is primitive, charmed, charged, affective. Only secondarily is it conceptual and derivative. From a different angle, and through a different process, the philosopher Maurice Merleau-Ponty knew this thing, and I would recommend anyone who cares about such matters to read his amazing *Phenomenolgy of Perception*. I myself have arrived at such convictions through years of devotion to its untapped capacities for expressiveness, its recalcitrance, its elusiveness. I believe like Maurice Blanchot that "language is possible because it strives for the impossible." And "the poet is nothing but the existence of this impossibility, just as the poem is nothing but the retention, the transmission of its own impossibility." There is a way of conveying meaning beneath the level of the meaning of the words themselves, and this for me is where the true capacities and powers and charms and seductions of language reside. Language works on one in some of the same ways music does. It shapes silence. Through an arrangement of tones and rhythms, against a shimmering backdrop of silence, music can produce subliminal, physiological, psychological, emotional, and sometimes mystical responses. The effect of key, the press of syllable, the modulation of tone, the vowel's drawl, the rhythm of hip and word and world, the flick of the tongue, or the heat of the hand can create sublime and profound states. I am hoping in a series of books like this one to explore the erotic through the thoroughly incarnate medium of language. I am hoping to get closer to my own desire. I am imagining free. Free some day.

In this preliminary work desire has informed and shaped diction and syntax. It has shown me how to determine the line, the paragraph. It has intimately influenced not only the trajectory of the narrative but its very definition. Desire insisted at times on a kind of formlessness, indeterminacy, excess. A series of intensities without objective. Plans are abandoned, resolutions are broken, preconceptions fall away. Desire does not follow but rather distorts and warps the usual unities and coherencies, and some of the stabilized notions of self and other. I have let it determine my notion of "character" and the treatment of time. It is responsible for the various swellings and verges and delays and elongations and collapses—it has brought a certain wildness, vibrancy, immediacy I have found somewhat lacking in my work. *Aureole* begins, but only begins, to explore writing as another kind of lovemaking, and lovemaking as another kind of writing.

Line by line I have tried to get closer to an erotic language, a language that might function more bodily, more physically, more passionately. Enjambment, flux, fragmentation, the elision of the object, the detached clause, the use of arpeggios, a changing dynamics, dangling participles, various aphasias— the unfinished sentence, or the melting of one sentence into another, the melting of corporeal boundaries, the dissolving of a subjective cohesion—these are some of the strategies I have attempted here. For the most part they were done intuitively as I tried to surrender and enter a sexual reverie on the level of language. Blurrings, changes in focus, and contradictions abounded. The oxymoronic, the parabolic appeared, serving as—well, who knew?—perhaps as fortification against the dissolution, or a warning, of what might happen if one strayed too far from story. I have tried to explore a little the zones of speechlessness one sometimes enters during sex, the field of silence, the tug of it, the language voids and vacuums, the weird filling in with words. This called up Stein for me and her particular brand of playfulness—her baby talk, her repetitions, her abstractions, her songs. Her sense, her senselessness. The small codes, hopes, love letters she embedded in her texts.

In the strangeness of that emptying, then empty space, odd things came to the fore or swirled around that weird vortex I tried to fill up with nonsense, odd fragments of memory, with games from childhood (You are as light as a feather/As stiff as a board), hurtful games (she loves you not), with grand pronouncements, lies, small intimacies, with playfulness (violet-breasted, Poodle Basket), and other linguistic hijinks (She lifts her hips to her thirst and vice versa).

I have wanted a little of the way lovers sound, their sputterings, their hopeless stutterings, their confessions, what is most precious to them, the specific ways they are intimate—their ability to answer questions that have not been asked ("a lot of practice"). The direct plea asserting itself, the interruptions, the intervention of thought with sensation. This sentence from "Exquisite Hour" starts as a meditation and ends as a kind of urgent instruction: "The effect of key don't change it." I have played with changes in tense within a paragraph and sometimes within a sentence in order to capture that warped sense of time. I have worked with imprecision and with abstraction in order to mimic the varying tempos of perception, consciousness, lucidity as we sometimes near the sacred. A slow coming to marks the beginning of "Anju flying." Sleep and sex-drugged, dream-ridden, the images are kept deliberately fuzzy or vague as they come and go into focus.

There are point-of-view changes within paragraphs and sometimes sentences. Quick shifts in subject occur, as invariably one lover will call up a past love or experience, or fantasy will intermingle with reality, disrupting the more usual ways of thinking. The enlargement of a small detail which results in the loss of the whole, the blurring of the greater picture, the strange erasures of self, of place, and that other thing—is that you snow ghost?—which remains. Changes in perspective. How small and how far off the world seems all of a sudden. The trees like smoke....The attendant sadnesses, insights, dizziness, revelations. I've become more and more interested in trying to near the most ambiguous and ephemeral and fleeting states—"Anju giggling hope elusive stay awhile."

I have experimented with using language at a slight remove from its literal meaning—setting words free to act on each other in different ways. I have delighted in the pleasuring of the image by repetition or recurrence: "good girl's knot." The reiteration of the odd phrase ("some jumper cables") that asserts itself and floats, existing mysteriously and autonomously in a text or above a bed. "In the liminal space." The image culled from hallucination: "a line of girls in communion clothes." The trust in the outlandish or off image. The creation of a place for "ovoid, opalescent, lunate," in these pages. Such words stay with me much in the same way sensation remains in my body long after the lover has departed. The prolonged pleasure of language. "Clavicle" or "striped shirt" will set me to shudder long after because of the mark it's made on the mind. "Bleary chalice." I may relive this language experience later—"the way the lip clings...."

I've tried to work closely with sound: the texture and friction of dissonance, the lull, the consolations of rhyme—or the sinister and constraining qualities of rhyme in a piece like "Dreaming Steven." The derangement of syntax—to get closer to that tumult and disarray and disorientation. One of the greatest pleasures so far has been exploring the sexual energy of the sentence: "As bleary, delirious, the sound of bells, they make their way to the end of the long beach and sentence, far." I have begun to feel the erotic surge of the phrase, and have started to think more and more about how those insistences and urgencies might dictate the shape of a line. Poets, of course, are quite adept at such things, but it has taken me, the prose writer, a long time to get here. I love the ability to create new logics, a logic of passion, a logic of the body dramatized by where the line breaks, or the paragraph, a logic of passion created in the caesuras, in the gaps, where unexpected tensions or emphases can produce effects which are, to me at any rate, quite startling. A physical gathering of linguistic force might send the reader upward where finally all the pressure is brought to bear on an unlikely and startling word or phrase. Sounds pretty sexy, don't you think? Faltering, one stumbles perhaps, regains a kind of equilibrium and in the process enters a different realm. A realm where physical actions replace, or erase, thought ("downward stroke"). In an attempt to capture some of these swells I've tried to begin using punctuation to syncopate, much like a jazz musician, confident in her craft, conversant, in the hopes of bringing new pressures to bear, and also new places of release—so that a piece might tremble or shimmer or languish, surprise. I have wanted to reclaim punctuation from the prose writers a little. Liberate it, and myself. Have it make sense again. When the last double periods are placed on the lightkeeper's last matins I want to try to feel that finality, that force. To understand that there may be an instance where the parenthesis can never close. I want one day to get that right—to feel that vulnerable on the page, that bed of language, that world. Use of the upper and lower case too are meant to try to capture erotic surges, the press of the sexual, or the flow of emotion. The sentence staggered, breathless, lapsed or desperate. The sentence insistent or lingering. The sentence reinvented—dear Gertrude. The sentence as incantation.

As for the larger motions within the pieces, desire has been the inspiration and guide there as well. Many attempts have been made to try and get closer to that yearning, that longing through narrative decisions. In "Sappho Sings" I have tried to ride the crests and swells of delirious language-making, the excess of it, the surfeit of language, visions, ideas, wishes. To simply get lost in the sensuousness of language, just to enjoy it, feel it in one's mouth—to relish its gorgeousness. Insatiable. To enjoy the fluidity of one getting lost in the other. I have tried to stay near to the kinds of audacities and recklessness and strange rigors that desire creates—the dizziness. As if hurling myself off a precipice. In "Exquisite Hour" waywardness, dis-orientation becomes the narrative imperative. I am extremely interested in the incoherencies of desire, and this piece is inco-herent, it wanders off—going far afield, shifting point of view and place without preparation. Images are strange and height-ened; lines drop off or melt into one another to produce a lapsed, dissipated quality. There is an eerie and for me heart-breaking holding on and letting go simultaneously. I stumble here in this blizzard of language and narrative unable to know exactly what's going on in the blur—"Is that you snow ghost? Is that you candy gram? Strange visitations." This I am certain of: desire does not make a well-made short story. It makes you rethink closure, that's for sure.

In "Dreaming Steven" erotic fantasy informs the motions. Quick changes of position: physical position, language posi-tions, positions of the mind are the given. The constant need for novelty, replacement, substitution, multiplicity, simultaneity, the desperate lust for more or different images, the loopy, idiosyncratic needs: "fish in their mouths." The dark hilarity I have only begun to explore that often inadvertently exists in sexual fantasy. The elaborate and often comedic stagings in the theater of the mind. The artifice: the props, the funny colored lights, the costumes, the makeup. The flirtations with death, the jovial rehearsals for it—its seductive proximity and our desire for it. The thousand resurrections and reinventions. The demented jingles—its sweet, sweet music. Replenishments. Reinforcements. The refreshment. The courage afforded.

I love the insistence and tenacity of desire, the reiterations and rephrasings, the eternal returnings. The obsessiveness of the erotic imagination. The press and relentlessness of the vision: "the pier collapsing." The aching dissonances. The constant pushing of the voice up a notch, forcing the tone, changing the pitch, forcing the repetitions in a kind of extraordinary need, want, desperation. I am thinking specifically here of the "You Were Dazzle" pieces. And the shift in the construction of the recurring phrase "You were flowers in a barrel" to "You were flower petals floating in a barrel" which signals the move away, through the linguistic gesture as much as anything that is understood on the literal level. In fact, to my ear the literal statements, "you were never again," etc., sound like the kind of grand statement indicating that the obsession is far from over. But in the quieter "you were flower petals floating," the subtle shift carries a message and makes me think that just perhaps....A slight letting go of the obsession in a line like that begins to happen. The unconscious shift there tells me that just maybe....Not to say on another day the lover will not have returned at the height of the obsession one more time. In a way the two "Dazzle" pieces are meant to be read on a kind of eternal loop. And in "Her Ink-Stained Hands" what interests me is the holding back, the taking away, the terrible truncated shapes left without any real means to complete or resolve themselves. The fear that has calcified and assumes a kind of permanent stance.

Time as conventionally conceived in much fiction loses its meaning when placed in desire's crucible. Desire's temporality is not that generally of development, direction, or movement. Often, the erotic stops or suppresses time, and this is one of the notions I try to explore. Sometimes it warps time, sexual consciousness seeming to inhabit an odd hanging space. "In the passage between day and night. The transition. In the uncertain hour. In the time, you who are French speak, and I am able to attach a meaning to what you've whispered, as you approach me for the first time at the airport." That odd kind of tripped-up time where threads of thought, memory, sensation are all combined, dissolving the ordinary distinctions and boundaries in a kind of perceptual synesthesia. Only later can things be sorted out—and it is at this later point I believe that most writing, with its sense making, begins. But narrative here is far more diffuse; it's an altogether different kind of energy field. I have tried to enter the continuous present of the erotic experience—a present which is constantly unfolding and includes past and future in its fluid hold. Time is experienced, to borrow from Heidegger, as a "sequence of nows." That the past or future is autonomous seems not quite believable in this hanging, eroticized state. How to distinguish where the past leaves off and a present begins? When have we begun the future? In "Make Me Dazzle" there is the intermingling of time that allows the longing woman on the beach to converse in two time periods simultaneously to two different people in the simple: "you're right here." Other questions arise. Where do the lovers leave off and I, the writer, begin? Where does the life begin and the writing stop? But I am getting a little ahead of myself. What seems evident to me when thinking about time—and sexual desire pushes the issue—is that the now-routine way of calling up the past through the use of the flashback is disassembled here and rejected as an unviable and untruthful strategy. All formulas are suspect. Desire is not formulaic, lust is not formulaic, only pornography is. For me, many highly accepted and completely integrated and "cherished" devices, including the flashback, resemble nothing as much as themselves: accepted and recognizable storytelling devices of literary fiction and now staples as well of mainstream filmmaking. An agreed-upon way to shape reality. It reminds me of those traveling players in "Anju Flying Streamers After" who try to cobble together a bit of a scaffolding, jerry-build a clunky, makeshift structure so as to impose a bit of order on the disorderly, uncontrollable erotic life and death force.

I think of Lautréamont and his radical project in *Maldoror,* as he tried to expose and destroy simile and analogy. I think of his flagrant parodying of the novel at the end of that work. His irreverence. His dark joy. I take courage there.

I have given up any conventional notions of the novel in *Aureole.* I have tried to respect and indeed encourage the longing and the genuine mystery which exist between the discrete pieces. The hope is that this desire might augment, echo, and speak to the other motions of longing in this work. The figures from piece to piece are connected peripherally. An erotic consciousness of abundance and allowance, a kind of promiscuity, seems to allow them to move back and forth between space and time more readily than might otherwise be the case. Linguistic relationships seem freely transferable as well—floating through texts more as light comes and goes with its gleaming and ephemeral touch. As in electronic writing, which I find a highly charged and essentially erotic space, I have, from time to time, here attempted the splitting off of narrative or linguistic instants to both accentuate and dramatize the nearness and the farness of the various language and narrative constructions, with the hope of refining those proximities and creating new forms of yearning. Desires I was not even aware I had surfaced during the writing of these pieces. The true miracle of form.

I have chosen with some deliberateness the moments at which to hold each piece on the page. I have thought it most effective to allow them to exist in the hovering place—"in the night and glisten and holy water basin." In moments of arousal and suspension and vulnerability. Open. That Tantric state when the intertwined couple captures the moment right before *jouissance* and extends it into forever. To my mind, this work is a novel at the very moment of its forming, before the ordinary assignments are made, and with those assignments a necessary imposition of design, authority, dissimulation, and distance. I have tried, not entirely successfully I think, to keep the material nearest to its longing. At the place where there is no fixed central figure, no plot in the ordinary sense, temporality without chronology; the place of all potential. The book is in a state of ravel and unravel to me, forming before our eyes, grouping and regrouping, gathering and dissolving. At the periphery of the more expected book lies this one, at the edge of the more obvious and stable book. On the horizon of story, before the shapes are made manifest, and the connections lose their tenuous, mysterious, human hold. I have tried to leave this work at the most erotic moment, the most vulnerable and open. *Aureole* for me exists forever on the verge, on the edge of a slightly heightened and unhinged world, just before the narrative strands coalesce. Ordinary story seems rather false, and indeed a bit preposterous under the circumstances. It is derailed, detonated, overwhelmed by the intensity of sexual desire. Plot cannot be contained given the subversiveness and potential extremity of the subject. Content insists on its form here. It is my hope that at the book's threshold the reader and the writer might be allowed to inhabit an extended moment of suspended sexuality where anything might occur. In the moment "before the woman in Paris becomes anything she wants to be yet." In the moment before "whatever will happen next will happen." In "the liminal space, in the gap...." To float like the couple in the changing room, that unreal, crystalline chamber, "in some of their clothes," "in the just March."

Who has conjured whom here? One more time I begin to question my notions of the real. Some part of me is still in Paris and I look up to the beautiful floating window written in wrought iron, the astounding calligraphy of its balcony, to where the woman, when she is French, opens *The Fourth Book of Desire* or *The Book of Good-bye* once more. Set into a delirious language motion, sex motion, in the hovering, luminous afternoon. Today it seems from her all else has been spun. On another day, based on my reading, or my mood, or my desire for the text, it might be Sappho, beached on that lilting nymph who dreams the rest of *Aureole*'s cast into creation. What do we know of what she wrote or saw in the place where the papyrus tore? Or perhaps it is the woman who writes on the sheets. Who has conjured little Anna, trembling in the fire garden—

walking away from almost everything—and then finally from everything....Are these aspects of the unfolding self? Shall they ever find each other? Or is that not it at all? Where do I, Carole, exist in all of this? I cannot tell you the longing these figures bring up in me—each of us rising out of the other's want, each in dialogue with the other—as I attempt to live a little more through the openness and fluidity of the form. Do the women on the winter beach dream Steven? Or has he in his solitude and need created them? Will he ever know the opium addict who has left her bleary snow globe on his mantle? And Anju through veils...Stay awhile. A woman holds a child in her arms. Where has she come from? Where has she gone?

"...streamers flying after."

True, there is no central character moving through conflict making its more or less linear journey here; but rather a spectrum of consciousness, refracted, escaping and elusive, casting light and shadow in all directions. The potential in us, and the extraordinary, awesome potentials still asleep in the language. *Aureole* to my mind is the story of a woman who wants. A woman, free, before the author's final prescriptions. In the erotic, the notion of a stable, static being developing in the traditional ways makes little sense except as some kind of agreed-upon convention of legibility. I have only begun in this book to look for the places in the text where passion might yield another kind of logic, offer a different way of proceeding. *Aureole* remains a mysterious book to me. And the woman.

How will I find her—without a recognizable plot? How will I find her—as she changes shape and place, without warning? How will I recognize her as she wanders through every

genre—that passionate terrain? Where will I garner enough
trust, enough faith? How will I ever locate her without the
usual landmarks? How will I find her as she blithely moves in
and out of obscurity, of shadow and light? Again, the writing
asks me to be a better, a braver person than the one I know
how to be. None of the usual markers to hold onto. I am interested in how different as a process this work has been from
the way I once worked. In my earliest novel, *Ghost Dance,* I
followed a vision of an utterly mysterious woman into a kind
of comprehensibility. But in *Aureole* the tables have turned.
Who is that woman on the bridge who in different places and
guises continually reappears? In the beginning of this project,
I thought I knew; by the end I have no idea. A woman moving
along the relentless trajectory of her desire, transformed over
and over by it. I see works that will be called novels in the
future with a notion of character that is much more mutable.
I believe notions of plot as well will be radically reimagined—
and become much more open again. This is what art does
for me: It opens new places; it affords glimpses not glimpsed
before. Without it I not only fail to live fully, but I begin to die.
All too aware of the loss, I become a mourning thing.

I have tried to create a vibrant, spacious landscape where I
might live. A space that is generous in its allowances. A room
of my own—part prose fiction, part prose poem, part journal,
part notebook, part memoir, part song, sometimes part biogra-
phy. None of these forms alone quite meets the dimensions
or urgencies I have begun to feel. No one shape quite meets
the requirements of my desire. I have needed, I have wanted
everything—probably too much. Desire has forced me into
odd contortions, new constructions, a more unarticulated and
primal space, filled with primitive recollections—notions of

light and dark, hot and cold, birth and death, danger, fire, flood—memories of clearings, of harbors, tremor, convulsions as they press their way into language. Tracks in the snow.... When you came to visit me that night you left your enormous footprint in the ice. By the morning it had dissolved—and you. Shapes and forms that far from constricting or defining will be evocative, calling up the history of this ancient place, the memory of survival, the immediacy of hand, pulse of blood, the heat of the intellect, all that is beautiful, all that is still possible (intimations more and more often now of the South of France that sun-drenched...).

Without apology, I have tried to create something of a feminine space. New kinds of intimacies. I do not believe in the myth of ungendered writing. Luce Irigaray is much better than I am on this. She says: "Only those who are still in a state of verbal automatism or mimic already existing meaning can maintain such a scission or split between she who is a woman and she who writes. The whole of my body is sexuate. My sexuality isn't restricted to my sex and the sexual act (in a narrow sense). I think the effects of repression and especially the lack of sexual culture—civil and religious—are still so powerful that they enable such strange statements to be upheld as 'I am a woman' and 'I do not write as a woman.' In these protestations there's a secret allegiance to the between-men cultures." It is essential, I believe, for women to make their own shapes and sounds, to enact in prose and poetry and all other genres and in all other mediums, their own desire, and not just mimic the dominant forms. We must refuse to emerge already constructed. "The master mouthing masterpiece." Obviously this is a lot easier said than done. First, because it is difficult and still largely theoretical, and second, because it asks us once

again to marginalize ourselves, return to the periphery, just
as we are acquiring a recognizable speaking voice (theirs)
and being rewarded for doing it so well. Just as we are being
embraced—even if it is a conditional embrace. And yet...I like
to think of Hélène Cixous at times like this. She writes: "We
must work. The earth of writing. To the point of becoming the
earth. Humble work. Without reward. Except joy."

Except joy.

I have tried to make a place where pleasures and arousals
spread in a lateral radiance, in a kind of prolonged ecstatic. In
an aureole of desire. At once diffuse, specific, and inclusive. A
place where what is often discarded as unusable will be kept.
A place at once interested in the abstract, distant, and also the
utterly urgent, personal, even confessional. A place where we
do not have to apologize. A place of forgiveness. I have incor-
porated, taken into the body of this book, my own past work.
That there might be a place where we wouldn't have to disown
ourselves, loathe ourselves in that mild, insidious way, feel
ashamed of who we are, or who we were—ashamed by the one
who was younger, played it more safely perhaps, made even
more mistakes. To embrace our own texts, our written texts,
and the texts of our lives. To risk the things they love to call us
most: self-indulgent, histrionic, irrational. Indulgent, excessive,
pleasure texts—unconcerned with getting to the point. In love
with freedom. To walk out of the constraints of perfection, or
modesty, or approval, or taste, or integrity as integrity has too
often been defined. To escape the burden of the already-con-
structed and received forms—like the props and scaffolding
those traveling players cobble together in hopes of staging
the story of the bursting, uncontainable Anju—their efforts,
slightly funny, kind of wonderful, a little pathetic, sweet, naive,

creaking, and ultimately useless. And this is how I regard the old fictions. I want something else. I want there to be space enough for all sorts of accidents of beauty, revelations, kindnesses, small surprises. A space that encourages new identity constructions for the reader as well as the writer. New patterns of thought and ways of perceiving. New visions of world, renewed hope.

I have tried to create a space neither fictive nor autobiographical where I am allowed to exist in an utterly different way. Not as a character or through character, and yet not as author either. "Once again sadness has caught you off guard," a voice says in "Exquisite Hour." I have no idea who is speaking, it might be the drugs, or the desire, or the fencing master or a party guest—but I do know who is being spoken to—alas. It is me. Once again sadness.

In a piece I am working on now which shall appear in the next book, I have let my mind and body exist at such an angle to the subject that I am allowed to inhabit the material in a way that affords me a new place in the text. A question arises, painfully, acutely, through the text, and not in the voice of the character, and not in my own voice, and not in an "authorial" voice. A question I in any other guise would not have the courage or ability to pose: *Where does your life go?* The piece somehow has allowed me to ask the essential, unbearable question at the center of my fear. Because of the time it takes to make money I may not get to where I need to go. Overwhelmed, panicked, utterly dispirited by my day job. There has been no way to approach such a thing. But the text has allowed me to face it. This is perhaps the most difficult thing of all to describe. Through the urgency and force of my desire and through the open place desire has created in me I may enter my work and be engaged in ways that up until now have been off-limits. There is a different engagement—and the stakes finally start to make a little bit of sense.

Another interesting thing: For me there is less and less of a distinction between writing and living, and this work has clarified that. But that does not quite say it. Let me ask Woolf for help here. She says, "The test of a book (to a writer) is if it makes a space in which quite naturally, you can say what you want to say.... This proves that a book is alive: because it has not crushed the thing I wanted to say, but allowed me to slip it in, without any compression or alteration." As I was finishing *Aureole* I happened to hear on the radio that Marguerite Duras, one of the presiding angels of this text, had died. If there had not been room enough in the body of my work to honor her, I would have considered this work to be a failure, a book that failed to live on the most basic level. What would my writing be worth then? If on that March day completing "In the Last Village," there had not been made a place for her? The creation of an inclusive place—a viable and flexible internal and external space, much like sexual space, at once immediate and remote, completely mundane and utterly sublime —that is what I am after.

(I want to go as far as we went that afternoon in that room in the trees, our bodies filtering leaves and sunlight—the shapes on the wall—that odd, tripped-up time, the hum of early summer—to let in that kind of pleasure, that kind of light. A line of girls appears—you were always such a child— then disappears. You are long gone—except here. Right here. And then you are gone again. But I will not close the parenthesis yet...

The tenacity of the erotic.

I am on a train, as I always seem to be these days, and walking down the aisle I stop to look at someone lying stretched out on two seats, who must have looked like you because standing over this innocent figure I whisper, *wake up now.* What has brought you here to me? The motion of the train? The desire in these pages, as I finish up the last revisions to *Aureole?* What has provoked such emotion, such delusion? Who has brought you here? Could it really be you? The movement of the train, does that have something to do with this delusion, this emotion? And the fact that I know you are afraid to fly and that you must be doing a lot of traveling lately and that you travel by train whenever you can, and because you are tired—sleeping in fact, as I stand over you in motion, scribbling, whispering—I try not to think of myself this way...

My desire to awaken you, and us, retrieve you again, and us, seeing you now as I do before me. You are in the midst of your fifteen minutes of fame and there is not a place, quite suddenly, I can turn without seeing your face—a face I have not seen in years now; there is not a mouth who is not saying your name— or so it seems. And as I write over someone quite asleep, desiring, longing to have you with me (that Amtrak bathroom), to keep you with me—even this sleeping version of you—though you have gone for what is probably forever—trying even here, in the most inappropriate of places, an essay for God's sake— the elongation of the sentence, to keep you here—not allowing the pen to lift from the paper—to make the words, run on and on, in the terrible, too small—and yes of course, I notice as I stand there that I try in language, using every resource, every strategy to have you with me again. I dreamt that floating train carried us and the narrative. And those words, once broken off with some violence, resumed. At least for a minute.

I want to get closer to sexual abandon in language, erotic wonder, spiritual awe. I want to be pressed up close to the speechlessness—as we form our first words after making love, having come back from that amazing and sacred place. I want to live next to the impossible, next to that which forever escapes us, eludes us. *Aureole* is small progress. But the book I love is the book it suggests—and it sends me back again into my own desire and want. This, all this too, and why not this and more and yes. That is the kind of book I wish for. Always more.

More. I'd like fountains in the text, gardens, reflecting ponds, zones of peace. Deep space. Fleeting, unlikely moments. A place where a clock sounds. A woman sings in French. Her voice caresses the overcast. A child presses her hand against the glass. I see her breath on the pane. She draws a heart. I'd like more weather. The press of cypress against stone, rain at the lip of the rose, she sings, listen, something about the snow....Charcoal gray graffiti and erasures on ancient stone. Prayers. Intimacies. What they whisper to each other on the rue Christine. The touch of sunlight, the way the hope comes and goes. The Seine running through me still— clinging still. I'd like there to be more swellings, more flooding in the texts. Abundances. More glances and glimpses, more tremblings. I want more hilarity, more bawdiness, more lust, pieces that are rougher around the edges. I'd like, as Cixous would say, more earth. More bloodstorm and sea ache, more birdsong, small warblings. More shimmer and lull. More electricity, fever. Many hotels and boats. I'd like there to be more silence, more darkness. More magic. Made-up languages perhaps; a place of babble. More memory of the sort that the body stores, and the memory that lives in the language. I'd like to pleasure the language for a long time yet, venerate, adore it.

Worship the visionary, mystical, ecstatic alphabet—I'd like to get a little closer to what that might mean. So much desire.... Between the night and the night. Between the god and the light—before we are asked to say good-bye. Must be an angel, I think...or Paris...or maybe Paradise....I'd like a lot of things. This is early work, I know. And I'm still a long way off. I recite a line by René Char to myself: *bring the ship nearer to its longing.* This book was written in offering to the book just out of reach—radiant, waiting.

The Re-introduction of Color

Stitch into your crimson dress a rose, a bowl, a code.
Stitch into your beautiful dress a sentence of your own—
a room into which one day you will walk.

for Joan Einwohner

ONCE I ROAMED IN BLINDING GREEN. White punctuating the scene. Dandelions in August. Blow on them and they would disperse and scatter their seeds. Brilliant yellow the next spring.

I was drenched in sunlight. Golden seemed to make a sound. Happy, dreaming, lilting child. Look at her, roaming as she is now toward her next adventure, in a place of wonder, iridescence. A green dock. Poodles on a jumpsuit. Beside a gray lake watching the sunfish—and their young, just hatched. You could almost scoop them up in your hands.

Once red flared from the corner of her world: a beach ball, a bird in winter, the roses her father grew. She felt orange, loved sage, the word indigo, a blue wave. A dock—that crystalline, floating feeling. Wildness of the child—her thousand enthusiasms. She tasted a red rose, pet the black swan that came to her, freed the fireflies her brother caught in a jar. Felt the terrible vibrations of the field against which that brother played—he's very ill. The child who loved the downbeat, stepped out of time—hearing the world that way. *Don't die.*

She loved being a horse perhaps most of all. She ran fast as the wind. A dark star blazed on her forehead. Running in clover, in heaths, o'er hill and vale—never mind it was suburban New Jersey, never mind. Limitation, like death, an unimaginable thing. Her heart beating wildly as she raced through every time and every terrain, *won't die, won't die,* her extraordinary, complicated tangle of mane, the nostrils flaring, the mouth and the eyes—devouring, the pounding of hoofs, universe, imagination on fire—the child. Utterly dizzied by the contours of the world—and the word. Its rhythms—its heat and light. Of everything there is to say and everything there is to do and be. The body's small but genuine heat— plowing through woods, hugging every tree. Dancing interpretive dances in her polka-dotted bathing suit, rattling a pod of seeds. In the idyll that was her childhood. Her mother at her side, a more than willing accomplice. *Look, Mother, a bird has fallen from its nest, look mother the rabbit's lair, look mother, oh look.* The child wandered freely. Hers the tendency to joy, to pleasure, irreverence, kindness, empathy, dream. The irresistible universe. A secret, a private place. She flew with arms extended once. She sang with fire. Made perfume from roses.

Dashed through water sprinkling brightly colored. Danced the can-can. Sang to summon the snow. Adored the rain. Made a May basket for her mother. Lined it with the moss from her special spot in the forest. Listened hour after hour to music with her father. Prayed for her brother, lighting candles on a secret altar: *won't die.* Begged the Virgin to appear. Dressed like a butterfly. Streamers flying. Staged elaborate puppet shows. Collected ladybugs. Tasted the night, felt the cat's velvet, memorized the sky. The stars seemed to make a sound like song. Twinkling. And in the day the sun rang like a bell sometimes. She raced to the edge of the known world. In freedom she imagined being anything, going anywhere. And if teachers or other forces tried to quell her enthusiasms early on—well, they were easy enough to ignore. In a wave, a star, a prayer, a made-up song, the swirl of her mother's dress—they were gone. Didn't they always want to reduce a complicated and terrible and terribly beautiful universe? If in those years there was someone anywhere near trying to rein her in or take any of it, any of it away, she did not notice.

A dark rose. A bottomless black cistern in which she wept. Prayed her made-up prayer. Made potions. Cast spells. A world of charms. Her life opening.

Imagine the shock then of late adolescence when the charms seemed to desert her, when everything she loved seemed to be taken away. Having roamed freely and unencumbered, the voices out of nowhere started demanding in a kind of staggered unison and from every direction the same thing—*conform, conform.* Abandon song, *conform.* Abandon reverence, *conform.* Surrender your freedom. Against nature, against intuition, *do something useful.*

How did she find herself suddenly estranged and at sea in an adulthood not of her own making? Exiled. For a time she must have tried to struggle against it—but like a butterfly pinned, trapped under glass, she felt her lovely wings as she pulled away from the pins to be disintegrating.

The hairline cracks already beginning to show during *the college years*. The stress of wanting to know what to do. The burden of a talent completely unrealized, utterly nebulous, just a pressing feeling, nothing even close to words on a page yet. And that strange counterforce coming from almost every- where. The message—*leave that all behind*—before she ever embraced it, or tried—*leave it behind*. Discouragement from every side. Even before she'd ever really begun. Good-bye.

Who is that sniveling baby who feels so terribly sorry for herself?

After the buffer of college where the struggle for the child's soul began in earnest. She stood smack up against the arrogance and demands of conventionality, its breezy assumptions.

And the request—to go quietly—don't make such a fuss about it.

A struggle of wills.

Having been raised to be an artist surely *of some sort*—even her mother now seemed to be defecting—*your writing*—some- thing to do *on the side perhaps?* She thought she was protecting her from heartache. Alas.

As she went from one tedious job in one awful law firm after another, she knew she was not going to come true. She was already mourning. She didn't even know whether there was any real writing in her—but the denial of the chance—the negation of. *Yes, but what have you written? Nothing, of course. Not much.*

Give up your childish notions, your silly daydreams. Hurry up, it's time. Conform, conform. Date. Marry. Work at a real job—not writing for Chrissakes—grow up.

In part it was this I suppose, in part something more— impossible to define, even now.

Look at that woman, once the ecstatic child, who walks slowly but undeniably further and further into her remoteness. Not so lonely—not so lonely there really.

A young person's struggle. She felt the terrible weight of convention on her and the magnitude of its demands. The methods were subtle ones—but the message was loud and clear—*give up your life for mine, step into line.*

Who is that woman who asks for one hopeful thing—and tries (it's a little pitiful) to console herself, or erase herself, or something —with recklessness, with sex, with anything she—what in the world is she wishing? A kind of rage, a fast moving inside, sur- feit of electricity in her head. And after awhile, after a few weeks usually—she would sink back one more time into speechlessness, dug deep and snug, it's dark in there, *she is, look, she is unable to lift a finger from the bed, or form a word— unable to form a word—oh yes, you'll be a writer some day!* The world flat and drained of color—only shades of gray and then and then—

E. M. Ciorin says, "The universe is a solitary space, and all its creatures do nothing but reinforce its solitude. In it, I have never met anyone, I have only stumbled across ghosts."

How to describe the place where the woman takes up resi- dence? She waves from the distance to the ones she loves, stranded now. Cut off. Frightened by the gap. How she still sometimes wanted to reach them, touch their faces, say their names, have a glass of wine with them perhaps. But the world was losing its vibrancy, its color, its feeling. She felt herself in a shroud of white. And how the sound seemed muffled. The snow—not possible to move through anymore. And the cold.

The remote hand holds the vestiges of the might-have-been —but forgetful, indifferent, or finally just too tired—you let go of it—that last recognizable part of you—you let it go. And you forget finally completely.

And she steps into numbness without much of a fight, without much of a fight after all. *Estrangement and distance become her, don't you think?*

Can't remember much anymore.

How to describe that white world where from time to time she might make small trips out into a terrible, animated rage, doing awful things, and then fall back into speechlessness, a sorrow so pervasive—*Is anyone there? Is anyone in there?* Doctors are saying, lovers are saying, friends are saying. Helen. Increasingly difficult. *Is anyone in there?* Increasingly difficult to know.

Once she did, she dreamed in brilliant green…Wildness of the child. Audacity of the child. That passionate, vibrant place.

Look we already know the artist is despised—and it's not too harsh a word, despised. *Really? You think you are a writer? Even if you were it would be treated with dismissal—(and you're no writer because, let's face it, a writer writes, does she not?)*

Of course the real contempt is reserved for the real writer, the real artist. She hears the scoffing of the bourgeoisie, the trivializing, the diminishing, the belittling of all that mattered most to her, whenever she'd come out for a little foray into the 1980s.

It is well past time to mention her father in all of this. The only one who purely encouraged back then. He was the only one as she moved toward adulthood who never asked of her or expected of her the typical, the conventional. Exerted no pressure. No will over her. The least patriarchal patriarch in the world. She should become an artist. Whatever that would mean. He had been a trumpet player, an artist—and he had felt, though he never said it of course, every day the gravity of disobeying that thing. He had been a musician—but now deprived of a sustainable art form (for how could a trumpet player with five children survive?) . He had withdrawn from the world. The price had been high. He lived in ice. She felt she was going there to join him.

Daddy.

Once the original, wild, insistent self is lost—how difficult it is to retrieve.

They lie in the amorphous dark and listen to music.

Somewhere she must have, certainly she must have still longed for that thing—wanting to hear as she once did—perfectly through water.

The parts that got lost.

She felt she was expected to follow the normative, asked, over time, since high school really, to put away the world's strangeness, its silences, its dark, its mystery and melancholy and fall into mindless, cheerful line—until the intensity of the strangeness—fear and awe, wonder and sorrow and everything you felt in silence, in the depth of your being, the power, the oddness, the truest, most important, original part of you— the part you could least afford to lose—was lost, socialized, little by little, almost entirely away.

She was asked to conform in absolutely every aspect of her life. Even when it did not appear so. Even in one's artistic choices—the place of so-called freedom.

Male editors at major houses are saying—female editors, who have embraced entirely the whole nine yards are saying:

Exactly what one should write. If you want to get published at any rate. And exactly how. So that even one's creative life was prescribed. In order to be published you must...orders coming down as if from on high. Place a character in a conflict and then resolve. Get the reader's attention through blah, blah, blah...Engraved on a kind of tablet. Serious fiction is. Serious fiction must. If you want to be reviewed. If you want to be taken seriously. If you want to publish with us. The promise of publication keeping everyone in some useless line. Everyone is gray and sounds the same.

Even the book is a box.

Do not take even this. Even this away. The one hopeful place. Even the book.

How to imagine shedding convention then? As insidious as it was, as ingrained. As ubiquitous as its message. Coming from every direction at once. What a novel is—what a family is—what a life is—what a woman's life must be—where was this voice coming from—it seemed it came from everywhere and nowhere at the same time. An admonishing figure.

All the diminishment. Her pale white universe. Slipping into a white shift, against white skin, and the hair prematurely turning white—*don't go,* someone whispers, but she can't do anything else really...

The thousand inappropriate ways one tried to get free back then.

The thousand less-than-perfect, oh yes, less-than-effective ways to try to wriggle free—or if not that—at least to forget a while.

I went to therapy finally as the result of an ultimatum. Helen said *go or I will leave you.* She said *someone could help you.* She said. And I could not fathom the idea of the world without her. She said. And because I loved her I said *yes.* Though she did not understand. Though I did not believe there was help for me. Though the very idea of therapy made me cringe—*all that talking*—I loved her. She said *we can't live like this anymore.*

She said, severely depressed, disoriented, out of control, she said. Suicidal. No, not that. It would have taken far more engagement I believed to have pulled off such a feat. Far more moral courage. Still it could happen perhaps—one liaison, one toxic narcotic cocktail away. I protested when she began the litany against me, but still I understood it as such: I was suffering, had been suffering a long time—in this time before real writing—when I was lost. A debilitating depression, a world hermetically sealed off—punctuated by episodes of high mania: sleeplessness, delusions, rage.

A string of sexual encounters. Did it not suggest I was still alive?

Get help.

Through the estrangement, through the isolation I could hear her—but muffled.

She said *or I will leave*

And that I had to go further and further, look for more and more elaborate, lavish, excessive, intense experience, more dangerous, more thrilling to prove—*to prove what?*

How had I gotten that way—that dangerously happy little girl, hour after hour, year after year, engrossed in her make-believe world? In love with the solitary place of her imagination.

She said. When the world was white and sorrow fell like snow, and nothing, nothing seemed familiar anymore.

And I said yes. Because my life had become utterly unrecognizable, not only to those who felt they knew or loved me, but also to me.

And on a day where the whiteness lifted, if only slightly, stumbling through drifts and drifts of oblivion in my pale shift, I went.

With real misgiving, trepidation dread even, a deep wariness. On an animated day I might have said how I detested psycho-babble, how skeptical I was of the whole endeavor. How suspect I found much of Freud—all the nonsense on women, on dreams. How hopeless, how useless. How much more clever I believed myself to be than anyone I could possibly find to work with. I went because I was forced to.

To the woman's office in her apartment on the Upper West Side. I sat glumly across from her. *I don't know what to say.*

Where to even imagine beginning? All that would be reduced or left out. Or overemphasized because language could best speak to certain things, but not others. The belief that words have stable meaning and can in ordinary speech convey what one is feeling struck me as naive and really quite quaint. And wasn't that how therapy was supposed to work? I was and am deeply suspicious of language, as I think any serious writer must be. My reverence for silence, and for what cannot ever be known or understood, made this therapy business a very dicey proposition indeed. The tendency to impose false shapes, the simplistic desire for the assignment of cause, one's hunger for why, one's need for motivation, then solution. The preconceptions, the generalizations, the summing up— all worrisome, worrisome. And the language—oh God— *dyfunctional* this and that, *empowerment issues, abandonment issues*—how awful. The one absolutely intolerable thing. The debasement of the language. I braced myself for the absolute worst.

Born in Paterson, New Jersey.

The oldest of five children.

Educated…

Have I mentioned my penchant for privacy, for solitude? *To be left alone.*

Who is that woman standing off to the side, so detached, so removed from herself, *narrating* the events of her life as if recounting another life altogether? Why is she so filled with caution, with reservation?

I was struggling against every stricture—it exhausts me now to think of. But it was more than that—it had always been more than that. Impossible to describe. Did I actually think that this very pleasant woman was ever going to be able to help me with any of this? Of course not.

That white world where I yearned to go forever. Never come back.

Why is she there at all?

The problem was I was hurting those around me including those I loved—there was the real problem. Was I hurting myself—not really—no, not intentionally. To break out of the habitual, the deadening—in expectation, in habit, in pattern, it seemed necessary to cause some violence, some harm to oneself. But not to others. I had been asked to go because of the damage I had done to others, and I went because I recognized that damage—and desired not to do that anymore. I wanted to be free, but not at any cost—to lose those I loved would be impossible—my last connections to this world. And of course, as it is now all too clear, I was not free in the least.

I go I suppose because I am unwell mentally, I do not say it, but dying in fact, I feel myself at twenty-six to be dying. In a stupor much of the time, with an impossible sadness—the grotesque, thudding afternoons, slow and dull, how to make them pass? Unable to speak, to rise, to move. For weeks and weeks sometimes.

And on other days, without middle ground, turned on a dime, without a break, I am so manic, so hyperactive and sick with it, so unable to focus, to sleep, to eat, filled with every delusion and plan; I am genius, utterly estranged, outside, writing such astounding work and so quickly, *works of art,* only when I look back at them to find page after page of virtually straight lines. Impossible, obviously, to even decipher. Let alone genius.

I seduce everyone in sight. Without much feeling. Going to the next adventure in search of someone or something to hold back the dead feeling. And it works. At least for awhile.

And the raining—what's that raining sound? Then snow. *Don't go.* Last bit of world. Last blue shadow.

Week after week I wrestled with it—if I could only describe to you, dear woman show you the contours of that world— drained of all color where I lay entombed, *Dr. E. I can't breath or move.*

Most people live lives of desperate accommodation I find. Overloved as a child I did not have the need to be loved or to please. I just wanted to live on my own terms.

Just.

Even the book is a box in this world.

First inklings of the box—of the dimensions of the thing—its shallow sides, its heavy lid makes a horrifying sound—and the early attempts to resist—there were signs early on—trouble early on in the refusal to assume the ordinary way of things: the prom, the driver's license, the National Honor Society—teenage rebellion? Yes, at the time it certainly looked that way. All the small refusals, the casual, seemingly casual, sloughing off of the prescribed identities, of the ways to behave.

Oldest sibling—but no role model, my sisters and brothers watched me in dismay. And entering the working world—appalled by the tedium and the language—that bantering all day long—that horrendous small talk—the clichés, the hundred abuses. I sat in mortal misery, suffering it—incapable of entering their various pacts.

Is she making sense? Is she making any sense?

The original self slowly usurped. Without exactly noticing at first. It was just a hollow feeling, a feeling of something being taken slowly away, pulled gently from you as you watched, half-cognizant but helpless. The wild self being normalized. How difficult to retrieve a life, once it is relinquished. One felt someone somewhere getting a sinister pleasure from this. *She is paranoid.* The more you balked, the more exhausted you became. All part of the plan.

My parents next to me—people I desperately loved—and yet could not follow. Their dreams and ambitions seemed to me not their own but something they had borrowed, a weird loan that they had accepted without much question. I loved them but could not love their assumptions. I would have to break their cherished, their given—not because I wanted to—

but in order to survive. It sounds perhaps melodramatic, but it was the terms of the struggle then.

The struggle against those forces was the fight literally for one's life. I sat across from her. *You are up to it,* she seemed to be saying. She gave me a taste for it. *Don't give up.*

And to not somehow fill that vacuum, that loss of coordinates with cynicism, disengagement, withdrawal, self-protection, guilt. Somehow.

We sat there together and circled it week after week, year after year. Through the thousand retreats and reversals and dismissals and setbacks.

As I walked yet again into another darkened bedroom, another alleyway—*begin again.* Back to my white world. *Begin again.* Back into the silence.

The struggle to freedom.

The struggle not to emerge already constructed.

To walk away from all oppression in full knowledge of the consequences. To live outside the usual tyrannies, conventions. To separate finally not from those one despises or is indifferent to—that is easy enough—but from the ones one most deeply loves—so as to be autonomous. To walk out of every enclosure. Fluent at last in your own language. One felt often in that room the strictures of language, the strictures of all existing forms: literary, emotional, social, political. The limits.

> *Put something down.*
> *Put something down some day.*
> *Put something down some day in my.*
> *In my hand.*
> *In my hand right.*
> *In my hand writing.*
> *Put something down some day in my hand writing.*

Those lovely lines of Gertrude Stein.

I was unable to live within the expected perimeters, tired of the usual assignments. I am more lucid about this now than I was then; forgive me, I do not mean to reduce or trivialize, and I do wonder whether it is therapy after all that has made it possible to say these things: facile, useful, but perhaps not entirely true.

I have been uneasy from the start about writing this piece. I am not a procrastinator and yet have put it off countless times. It troubles me. The danger of this kind of writing and of all writing to some degree is all too evident, all too present at every turn. And it in some ways resembles the dangers of therapy. What is this desire to become comprehensible to one's self? To net the escaping one, haul her in to dissect and understand and to finally display. The temptation, the risk is to assign meaning, motive, cause, in an attempt *to feel a little bit better.* Not so amorphous, not so out there. To fix the elusive self. To invent a character—and a role to play. The "I" stabilized, fixed on the page now, feigning illumination—What violence do I do to myself and to language, and to the magic of those afternoons with her? What did I learn there? What happened in that room? Well one can well understand the trepidation in writing any of it—What do I change or give up or alter in ways I may not even be aware of—what will I say here in the attempt to communicate something?

How improbable that she met me in snow offering a bouquet of brilliant reds and greens and gold—an offer to return—

Not possible.

Why not? she asked.

Her good sense. Her strange faith. Her practicality. It was a consolation like no other. Certain things could actually be done, could be controlled, demystified. When her colleague, a psychiatrist I had been sent to see, decided to try to seduce this seducer, seduce this basket case in the usual business-as-usual, garden-variety abuse of power, she reports him, without hesitation, to the proper people. Her clear-thinking, straightforward sense of things. One could not help but be impressed. She acts swiftly and without fanfare. And that is it.

And how, and I do not know how exactly—that Upper West Side address over time became a saving thing—a place to go—a place to look forward to in the way I look forward to that which is extremely difficult, challenging, and mysterious and essentially impossible—what I mean is—the way I look forward to writing.

How did she reach me in time? The charm of this life. How did I find her? This one particular woman—who never uttered a word of psycho-babble, who never pretended there were answers, who never displayed anything but wisdom and care.

Her cat, her sullen teenage daughter, her lovely husband, who would from time to time make appearances—the magic of those afternoons in that prewar Upper West Side building— it was a weird bliss—even when I left frightened, or in tears.

Never known such respite.

What was happening to me?

Here is a crimson dress.

Yes?

And I stepped out of my white shift.

A memory, a pressure. Color—in a world bereft of color. Red. Timbre of blue. Touch of ochre. The beloved world—a slow coming to.

I did not dare to hope. A memory of vibrancy. Step. Ascent. Motion. Memory of motion. Not dare. Memory of scent. Of collecting mosses in the forest. Plush. Green. Once she dreamed. Grace notes. Moments of grace. I did not dare. My father and I again in the moody Saturday afternoons listening to music. Every flower. Each and every. Blooming in the snow white of my mind's eye. Like a rose in winter opening.

Blue and red and gold brocade, stitch.

Streamers flying after.

Here is a wish, stitch.

What happened there?

Two women sitting together in a dark room on the Upper West Side of Manhattan on those days of bottomless misery when nothing seemed to give way.

We make a dress together. Something it might be possible to wear. Invent a room. And imagine somewhere it might be possible to live again.

There was safety there in that place with her, harbor, rest, comfort. Intimations of limitless possibility, integrity, pure health. Creating a place for one's deepest longings—a child perhaps, a piece of writing never seen before. The wanting comes back. It took years. All the hope. I scarcely can believe.

In that world completely drained of color we choose red. Here is a thread.

Pass the black line through the needle's eye and watch. Be patient. Here is a silver fish, a star, a sequin, released on a red velvet sea, swim to it. A bead of blue glass.

Two women in the perfection of the struggle. To be alive. One guiding the other. One older, wiser. Here is a strand of gold.

To live outside the thousand impositions. To live one's life without inordinate fear, without needless apology. To invent oneself from scratch, if necessary. Against a field of possibility. Against the promise of green.

Accretion of the afternoons, years. Time passes. Years pass. Something happens. Impossible to describe or quite understand.

That opening. That clearing in the woods.

Gertrude Stein: When she shuts her eyes she sees the green things among which she has been working and then as she falls asleep she sees them a little differently.

The incredible dimensions of her kindness and intelligence and discretion. Her compassion, her intuition, her open-mindedness. Utterly free of dogma or cant. The exact opposite of what the young woman expected, grimly waiting in that foyer the first day.

To examine calmly all the destructiveness—and to look at it as if from a distance—and not judge.

When the world is snow, is flat, is cold, when all you want to do is to lie down and die into it—step into that dress.

Stitch all your wishes, fears, and the words you love most. Inscribe a hope, a worry, a sentence of your own.

Embroider your name someday. In your own handwriting.

Yellow flowers—those were buttercups. *Do you like butter?* Running through a field of green.

No epiphanies, no closure, just patterns, trends, an inkling of a design. No reasons. The embracing of complexity, ambivalence, contradiction. No false crescendos. Only one's life *there, there*—stretched out before one—open again. Given back. Taken back. Those endless afternoons.

Blue and green and gold brocade. Feathers, bells, someday.

The soul's journey toward small light—the struggle toward freedom. The same journey I continue on now alone, as is necessary, as it must be.

I write every day—to be well. Have done it now for some time. Revel in it—the solace that comes from making shapes, the joy that comes from high seriousness, the humility I acquire at every turn.

It was the reach in that room Dr. E., that was so beautiful.

Is there any way I can ever let you know all that it meant to me?

How extraordinary to try and write oneself free. To live inside the language. The lifelong motion toward original expression. What an extraordinary way to spend one's little time here.

I know I have never been ordinary—not even back then—though I did not realize it of course. As I called to my mother whom I loved so much—*Mommy, Mommy,* it was as if from a great distance. I was always a little outside. It might have been a clue.

Human voices—they come, they die away.

Have I ever thanked him I wonder? I think I have not. My father with his unconditional love, and his unspoken, silent but complete support. My melancholy father, with his ghost trumpet, the only figure of genuine consolation—because he understood what the others could not—in this whole universe.

A few connections now—more than enough—Helen, my parents, a handful of friends…

And this. This luminous alphabet.

And oh how now the syllables move to round and soft, to coo and smooth. To safe. To dream. Look, how it is possible to invent one's life—on one's own terms—entirely—almost entirely. And I am happier than I have ever been—seven months pregnant today. How can I describe this state of grace?

Having finally moved through another construction, another constraint, as if through water and on to the other side.

Blue and green and sparkling. This miraculous life.

It was the reach in that room that was so beautiful.

Break Every Rule

REMARKS MADE AT BROWN UNIVERSITY'S
GAY AND LESBIAN CONFERENCE 1994 AND AT
OUTWRITE, BOSTON, MASSACHUSETTS, 1998.

*I*F WRITING IS LANGUAGE and language is desire and longing and suffering, and it is capable of great passion and also great nuances of passion—the passion of the mind, the passion of the body—and if syntax reflects states of desire, is hope, is love, is sadness, is fury, and if the motions of sentences and paragraphs and chapters are this as well, if the motion of line is about desire and longing and want; then why when we write, when we make shapes on paper, why then does it so often look like the traditional, straight models, why does our longing look for example like John Updike's longing? Oh not in the specifics— but in the formal assumptions: what a story is, a paragraph, a character, etc. Does form imply a value system? Is it a statement about perception?

If the creation of literary texts affords a kind of license, is a kind of freedom, dizzying, giddy—then why do we more often than not fall back on the old orthodoxy, the old ways of seeing and perceiving and recording that perception?

Why do we adopt the conventions of, for lack of a better word, the oppressor?

Is it because we've lost faith in our belief that language is capable of a kind of utopia, speaking to myriad versions of inner and outer reality?

Or is it that we on the margins long secretly for nothing more than to be embraced by the mainstream? To *become* the center?

Is it that we want the security, the emotional, the financial security that comes with those who tailor their visions or in some way comply with the *Agreement*.

If language is desire, if syntax and rhythm and tone and color create worlds of desire, if we see, if we live out on the margin, then how come we so often write between the lines? We who are ostracized, estranged, despised, denied rights of every kind? Why do we write as if we were inside?

I do not feel in the position to judge or understand the motives of my fellow gay and lesbian writers. I am only here to pose some questions.

Why does realism equal verity? And whose verity is this? Why does realism equal accessibility? Might there be ways outside the standard models that could afford both reader and writer a few more options? Accessible in whole new ways.

Would disrupting or upsetting the lexical surfaces, and the deeper structures disrupt other contracts (social, political) we have entered with those who have continually tried to dismiss us?

If we joyfully violate the language contract, might that not make us braver, stronger, more capable of breaking other oppressive contracts?

Might our pleasure, our delight, our audacity become irresistible finally?

Would celebrating through the invention of new kinds of texts—ones that insisted on our own takes of the world, our own visions, our own realities—would this finally convince both us and others that we are autonomous, we are not them, not exactly, but we are nonetheless joyful and free? In short we too are complex human beings and cannot be so simply reduced or read.

And what if that were reflected in our prose? All the things that matter most.

If through language, through literature, through what we make we refuse to accept our limitations, if we are wild and unruly and unswerving in our conviction and irreverence, will those who try to contain us get it finally?

Might the old novel, one day, like the old ways of thinking about gender and race and sexuality, simply appear silly, outdated, quaint?

Might writing by women, by people of color, by gay men and lesbians be an active refusal of the dominant code, a subversion of meaning as it has been traditionally constructed, for something perhaps more strange, elusive, other?

Carla Lonzi and *Rivolta Femminile* from "I Say I":

You would like to keep me under your guardianship.
I distance myself and you do not forgive me.
You do not know who I am and you make yourself my mediator.
What I have to say I will say on my own.

Rupture, Verge, and Precipice
Precipice, Verge, and Hurt Not

Be not afraid. The isle is full of noises,
Sounds and sweet airs that give delight and hurt not.
— WILLIAM SHAKESPEARE

You ARE AFRAID. You are afraid, as usual, that the novel is dying. You think you know what a novel is: it's the kind you write. You fear you are dying.

You wonder where the hero went.

You wonder how things could have gotten so out of hand.

You ask where is one sympathetic, believable character?

You ask where is the plot?

You wonder where on earth is the conflict? The resolution? The *dénouement*?

You imagine yourself to be the holder of some last truth. You imagine yourself to be in some sinking, noble, gilt-covered cradle of civilization.

You romanticize your *fin de siècle*, imbuing it with meaning, overtones, implications.

You are still worried about TV.

You are still worried about the anxiety of influence.

You say there will be no readers in the future, that there are hardly any readers now. You count your measly 15,000—but you have always underestimated everything.

You say language will lose its charms, its ability to charm, its power to mesmerize.

You say the world turns, spins away, or that we turn from it. You're pretty desolate.

You mutter a number of the usual things: You say, "…are rust," "…are void" "…are torn."

You think you know what a book is, what reading is, what constitutes a literary experience. In fact you've been happy all these years to legislate the literary experience. All too happy to write the rules.

You think you know what the writer does, what the reader does. You're pretty smug about it.

You think you know what the reader wants: a good old-fashioned story.

You think you know what a woman wants: a good old-fashioned—

You find me obnoxious, uppity. You try to dismiss me as hysterical or reactionary or out of touch because I won't enter that cozy little pact with you anymore. Happy little subservient typing "my" novel, the one you've been dictating all these years.

You rely on me to be dependent on you for favors, publication, $$$$$$$$$, canonization.

You are afraid. Too smug in your middle ground with your middlebrow. Everything threatens you.

You say music was better then: the Rolling Stones, the Who, the Beatles, Fleetwood Mac. You're boring me.

You say hypertext will kill print fiction. You pit one against the other in the most cynical and transparent ways in hopes we'll tear each other to bits

while you watch. You like to watch. Hold us all in your gaze.

Just as you try to pit writing against theory, prose against poetry, film against video, etc., as you try to hold on to your little piece of the disappearing world.

But I, for one, am on to you. Your taste for blood, your love of competition, your need to feel endangered, beleaguered, superior. Your need to reiterate, to reassert your power, your privilege, because it erodes.

Let's face it, you're panicked.

You think an essay should have a hypothesis, a conclusion, should argue points. You really do bore me.

You'd like to put miraculous, glowing glyphs on a screen on one side and modest ink on pretty white paper on the other.

You set up, over and over, false dichotomies. Easy targets. You reduce almost everything, as I reduce you now. Tell me, how does it feel?

You're really worried. You say sex will be virtual. The casting couch, virtual. But you know as well as I do that all the other will continue, you betcha, so why are you so worried?

You fear your favorite positions are endangered. Will become obsolete.

You believe you have more to lose than other people in other times.

You romanticize the good old days—the record skipping those nights long ago while you were making love, while you were having real sex with—

Hey, was that me? The Rolling Stones crooning: "I see a red door and I want it painted black, painted black, painted black…"

Want it painted black.

Or: "Brown Sugar, how come you dance so good, dance so good, dance so good…???"

You want to conserve everything. You worship false prophets. You're sick over your (dwindling) reputation.

You're so cavalier, offering your hand….

Jenny Holzer: "The future is stupid."

I remember the poet-dinosaurs that evening at the dinner table munching on their leafy greens, going extinct even as they spoke, whispering "language poetry" (that was the evil that night), shuddering.

You fear the electronic ladyland. Want it painted black.

You're afraid of junk food. The real junk food and the metaphoric junk food the media feeds you. Want it painted black...

painted black.

You fear the stylist (as you have defined style) will perish.

You consider certain art forms to be debased and believe that in the future all true artists will disappear. Why do you believe other forms to be inferior to your own?

You consider certain ways of thinking about literature to be debased. You can't decide whether they're too rigorous or too reckless, or both.

Edmund Wilson, Alfred Kazin, Harold Bloom *et fils*—make my day.

You think me unladylike. Hysterical. Maybe crazy. Unreadable. You put me in your unreadable box where I am safe. Where I am quiet. More ladylike.

In your disdainful box labeled "experimental." Labeled "do not open." Labeled "do not review."

You see a red door and you want it painted black.

No more monoliths.

You who said "hegemony" and "domino theory" and "peace with honor."

All the deaths for nothing. All the dark roads you've led us down. No more.

The future: where we're braced always for the next unspeakably monstrous way to die—or to kill.

All the dark deserted roads you've led me down, grabbing at my breasts, tearing at my shirt, my waistband: first date.

Second date: this is how to write a book.

Third date: good girl! Let's publish it!!!

Brown Sugar, how come you dance so good?

Fourth date: will you marry me?

You fear the future, OK. You fear anything new. Anything that disrupts your sense of security and self. Everything threatens you.

Where is the change over the course of the thing in the hero?

Where is the hero?

Where's the conflict? Where the hell is the *dénouement*?

I see your point. But haven't you asked us to write your fiction for just a little too long now? Couldn't we—

Couldn't we, maybe just possibly, coexist?

Why does my existence threaten yours?

It's been too long now that you've asked me to be you. Insisted I be you.

Lighten up. Don't be so afraid. Put up your hand. Say: Bunny, Alfred, Harold, bye-bye.

You fear. You fear the television. You loathe and adore the television.

You feel numbed and buzzed by so much electronics. Numbed and buzzed by so much future.

I'm getting a little tired of this "you" and "I." Still I am learning a few new things about you—and about me.

The future of literature. The death of the novel. You love for some reason, the large, glitzy questions and statements. But the question bores me—and all the usual ways of thinking and speaking and writing anymore.

I'm sorry you are so afraid. You want it to be something like the movie *2001,* the future. You want it to be ludicrous, the future, easily dismissable. Like me. If only I didn't dance so good. You demand to know, How come

you dance so good, dance so good, dance so good…???

You can't see a place for yourself in it and it frightens you. You dig in your heels as a result. Spend all your considerable intelligence and energy conserving, preserving, holding court, posturing, tenaciously holding on, now as you munch your last green leaves, yum.

Where is the resolution of the conflict? Where the fuck is the conflict?

What if a book might also include, might also be, the tentative, the hesitant, the doubt you most fear and despise?

Lyn Hejinian: "Closure is misanthropic."

Fear of growth, fear of change, fear of breaking one's own mold, fear of disturbing the product, fear of ridicule, fear of indifference, fear of failure, fear of invisibility, fear of, fear of, fear of....

You say that language will cease to be respected, will no longer move us. But we're already becoming numb thanks to what you are afraid to give up. What you flood the market with.

Soyinka: "I am concerned about preserving a special level of communication, a level very different from Oprah Winfrey."

Wish: that all talk-show fiction be put to bed now. Its fake psychologies, its "realisms." Its pathetic 2 plus 2.

Language of course has an enormous capacity to lie, to make false shapes, to be glib, to make common widgets, three parts this and two parts that.

Wish: that all the fiction of lies be put to bed.

That the dishonesty running rampant through much contemporary fiction be recognized as such.

What deal must I strike in order to be published by you? What pose, bargain, stance, is it I must strike with you now?

What mold do you make of me to pour your elixir, your fluid into, and then reward?

The bunny mold? The kitten mold? The flower mold? The damaged flower mold? Pregnant at twelve, illiterate, but with a twist? The gay mold? The white trash mold? The battered child mold? The bad girl mold?

Paint me black. Paint me Latina. Paint me Native American. Paint me Asian and then pour me into your mold. Use me. Co-opt me. Market me.

Debase me and in the future I shall rise anew out of your cynicism and scorn—smiling, lovely, free.

I know a place that burns brighter than a million suns.

Wish list: that the business people who have taken over the publishing houses will focus themselves elsewhere and leave the arts alone again.

Not to own or colonize or dominate. . . .

Despite all efforts to tame it, manage it, control it, outsmart it, language resists your best efforts; language is still a bunch of sturdy, glittering charms in the astonished hand.

A utopia of possibility. A utopia of choice.

And I am huddled around the fire of the alphabet, still.

Even though you say one word next to the other will cease to be cherished.

You say rap music is poison. Hypertext is poison.

Even though you call me sentimental—on the one hand girly-girl, on the other hand loud-mouthed bitch, on the one hand interesting and talented writer, on the other hand utterly out-of-touch idealist, romantic—it is you who wants the nineteenth century back again. When things were dandy for you, swell. You want to believe in the old coordinates, the old shapes. To believe in whatever it was you believed in then. You were one of the guys who dictated the story, sure, I remember. Who made up the story and now go teaching it all over the place. But even then, when you sat around making it up, even then, my friend, it had nothing to do with me. With my world. With what I saw and how I felt.

Wish: that all graduate writing programs with their terminal degrees stop promoting such tiresome recipes for success or go (financially) bankrupt.

Your false crescendos. Climaxes. False for me, at any rate.

The future is all the people who've ever been kept out, singing.

In the future everything will be allowed.

So the future is for you, too. Not to worry. But not only for you.

For you, but not only for you.

Not to discard the canon, but to enlarge it.

No more monoliths. No more Mick Jaggers. No more O. J. Simpsons. No more James Joyces. No more heroes.

Everything threatens you. Hacks, hackers, slacks, slackers, cybergirls with their cybercurls and wiles, poets of every sort. Rock bands with girls.

You believe your (disappearing) time represents some last golden age of enlightenment, to be guarded, protected, reproduced against the approaching mindlessness, depravity, electronic states of America.

But maybe as you become more and more threatened, you'll take a few more risks yourself. Who knows? Anything is possible in the future.

Wish list: that the homogeneity end. That the mainstream come to acknowledge, for starters, the thousand refracted, disparate beauties out there.

That the writers and the readers stop being treated by the mainstream houses like idiot children. That the business people get out and stop imposing their "taste" on everyone.

Wish: that as writers we be aware of our own desire to incorporate, even unconsciously, the demands and anxieties of publishers and reject them, the demands and anxieties of the marketplace.

That the business people go elsewhere.

Market me. Promote me. Sanitize me. Co-opt me. Plagiarize me. Market me harder.

Wish list: that the grade inflation for a certain kind of writing stop, and that the middlebrow writers assume their middle position so that everyone else might finally have a place, too. Be considered seriously, too. Be read, too.

Paint me black. Paint me Latina. Paint me Chinese. Pour me into your mold and sell me harder.

Fuck me (over) harder.

Those of us jockeying for position in the heavens, intent on forever, major reputations, major motion pictures and $$$$ $$$$, life after life after life after death, forget about it.

Wish: that straight white males reconsider the impulse to cover the entire world with their words, fill up every page, every surface, everywhere.

Thousand-page novels, tens and tens of vollmanns—I mean volumes.

Not to own or colonize or dominate anymore.

"Well, we've been kept from ourselves too long, don't you think?" an old woman in Central Park says to a friend.

Two women in the park at dusk.

Turn the beat around:

The pauses and rhythms and allowances of Laurie Anderson. The glow of Jenny Holzer. The ranting and passion of Courtney Love. Brilliance of Susan Howe. Brilliance of Erin Mouré. Theresa Cha. Visionary P. J. Harvey. Suzan-Lori Parks.

The future is feminine, for real, this time.

The future is Emily Dickinson and Emily Brontë and Gertrude Stein still. The future is still Maya Deren and Billie Holiday.

Language is a rose and the future is still a rose, opening.

It is beautiful there in the future. Irreverent, wild.

The future is women, for real this time. I'm sorry, but it's time you got used to it.

Reading on a train by the light the river gives. The woman next to me asleep. Two plastic bags at her feet. Lulling, lovely world. And I am witness to it all—that slumber—and then her awakening—so vulnerable, sensation streaming back, the world returned, the river and the light the river gives, return-ing language, touch, and smell. The world retrieved. I am privileged to be next to her as she moves gracefully from one state to the next, smiling slightly. I recognize her delight. It is taken away, and it is given back. The miracle and mystery of this life in one middle-aged black woman on the Metro North next to me. The Hudson River widening.

Let all of this be part of the story, too. A woman dreaming next to water.

The future: all the dreams we've been kept from. All the things yet to dream.

An opening of possibility. A land of a thousand dances.

I want sex and hypersex and cybersex, why not?

The river mysteriously widening, as she opens her eyes.

We can say, if we like, that the future will be plural.

Our voices processed through many systems—or none at all.

A place where a thousand birds are singing.

"The isle is full of noises. . . ."

A place without the usual dichotomies. No phony divisions between mind and body, intelligence and passion, nature and technology, private and public, within and without, male and female.

May we begin a dialogue there in the future. May we learn something from each other. Electronic writing will help us to think about impermanence, facility, fragility, and freedom, spatial intensities, irreverences, experimentation, new worlds, clean slates. Print writing will allow us new respect for the mark on the page, the human hand, the erasure, the hesitation, the mistake.

Electronic writing will give us a deeper understanding of the instability of texts, of worlds.

Print writing will remind us of our love for the physical, for the sensual world. And for the light only a book held in one's hands can give. The book taken to bed or the beach—the words dancing with the heat and the sea—and the mouth now suddenly on my salty neck.

Electronic writing shall inspire magic. Print writing shall inspire magic. Ways to heal.

"Intoxicated with Serbian nationalist propaganda, one charge is that X took part in the murder of a Muslim civilian, F, by forcing another Muslim to bite off F's testicles."

What is a book and how might it be reimagined, opened up, transformed to accommodate all we've seen, all we've been hurt by, all that's been given, all that's been taken away:

"...deliberately infecting subjects with fatal diseases, killing 275,000 of the elderly, the deformed and other 'useless eaters' through the guise of euthanasia, and killing 112 Jews simply to fill out a university skeleton collection."

No more monoliths. No more gods.

"Let us go then, you and I...."

No more sheepish, mindless devotion. No more quiet supplication.

All the dark roads you've led us down no more.

You will call me naive, childlike, irreverent, idealistic, offensive, outrageous, defiant at times, because I do not believe in a literature of limitation, in a future of limitation. I annoy you with this kind of talk, I know. You've told me many times before. You'd like me to step into my quiet box. You're so cavalier, as you offer your hand.

The future. Possibility will reign. My students poised on some new threshold. We're too diversified, we're too fractured, all too close in proximity suddenly—one world.

One wild world,

free of categories, free of denominations, dance and fiction and performance and installation and video and poetry and paint-ing—one world—every hyper- and cyber-

And in upstate New York, a woman sees fields of flax and iris and cattails, and dreams of making paper. And dreams of creating an Art Farm—a place just for experimenting with unusual indigenous fibers, a real space for bookbinding, an archive, a library, a gallery.

Dream: that this new tolerance might set a tone, give an exam-ple. This openness in acceptance of texts, of forms, this free-dom, this embrace will serve as models for how to live. Will be the model for a new world order—in my dream. A way to live together better—in my dream.

Godard: "A film like this, it's a bit as if I wanted to write a soci-ological essay in the form of a novel, and all I had to do it with was notes of music. Is that what cinema is? And am I right to continue doing it?"

But I do believe, and no doubt childishly, unquestioningly, in the supremacy of beauty, in pattern, in language, as a child believes in language, in diversity, in the possibility of justice—

even after everything we have seen—in the impulse to speak—even after everything.

"Peder Davis, a bouncy, tow-headed five-year-old, shook his head and said, 'I would tell him: You shoot down this building? You put it back together.

And I would say, You redo those people.'"

One hundred and sixty-eight dead in Oklahoma bombing.

"Peder said he drew 'a house with eyes that was blue on the sides.' He explained, 'It was the building that exploded, in heaven.'"

Wish: that writing again, through its audacity, generosity, possibility, irreverence, wildness, teach us how to better live.

The world doesn't end.

The smell of the air. The feel of the wind in late April.

You can't have a genuine experience of nature except in nature. You can't have a genuine experience of language except in language. And for those of us for whom language is the central drama, the captivating, imaginative, open, flexible act, there can never be a substitute or a replacement.

Language continually opening new places in me.

A picture of a bird will never be a bird. And a bird will never be a picture of a bird. So relax.

The world doesn't end, my friend. So stop your doomsday song. Or Matthew Arnold: "The end is everywhere: Art still has truth, take refuge there."

All will perish, but not this: language opening like a rose.

And many times I have despaired over the limits of language, the recalcitrance of words that refuse to yield, won't glimmer, won't work anymore. All the outmoded forms. Yet I know it is part of it, I know that now; it's part of the essential mystery of the medium—and that all of us who are in this thing for real have to face this, address this, love this, even.

The struggles with shape, with silence, with complacency. The impossibility of the task.

You say destined to perish, death of the novel, end of fiction, over and over.

But Matthew Arnold, on the cusp of another century, dreams: art.

And I say faced with the eternal mysteries, one, if so inclined, will make fictive shapes.

What it was like to be here. To hold your hand.

An ancient impulse, after all.

As we reach, trying to recapture an original happiness, pleasure, peace—

Reaching—

The needs that language mirrors and engenders and satisfies are not going away. And are not replaceable.

The body with its cellular alphabet. And, in another alphabet, the desire to get that body onto the page.

There will be works of female sexuality, finally.

Feminine shapes.

All sorts of new shapes. Language, a rose, opening.

It's greater than we are, than we'll ever be. That's why I love it. Kneeling at the altar of the impossible. The self put back in its proper place.

The miracle of language. The challenge and magic of language.

Different than the old magic. I remember you liked to saw women in half and put them back together, once. Configure them in ways most pleasing to you.

You tried once to make language conform. Obey. You tried to tame it. You tried to make it sit, heel, jump through hoops.

You like to say I am reckless. You like to say I lack discipline. You say my work lacks structure. I've heard it a hundred times from you. But nothing could be farther from the truth.

In spite of everything, my refusal to hate you, to take you all that seriously, to be condescended to—

Still, too often I have worried about worldly things. Too often have I worried about publishing, about my so-called career, fretted over the so-so-writers who are routinely acclaimed, rewarded, given biscuits and other treats—this too small prison of self where I sometimes dwell.

Too often I have let the creeps upset me.

The danger of the sky.

The danger of April.

If you say language is dying. . . .

Susan Howe: "Poetry is redemption from pessimism."

April in the country. Already so much green. So much life. So much. Even with half the trees still bare. Poking up through the slowly warming earth, the tender shoots of asparagus. Crocus. Bloodroot.

This vulnerable and breakable heart.

As we dare to utter something, to commit ourselves, to make a mark on a page or a field of light.

To incorporate this dangerous and fragile world. All its beauty. All its pain.

You who said "hegemony" and "domino theory" and "peace with honor."

To not only tolerate but welcome work that is other than the kind we do.

To incorporate the ache of Vietnam, the mistake of it, incapable of being erased or changed. To invent forms that might let that wound stand—

If we've learned anything, yet.

Summer 1885

Brother and Sister's Friend—

"Sweet Land of Liberty" is a superfluous Carol till it concerns ourselves—then it outrealms the Birds…
　Your Hollyhocks endow the House, making Art's inner Summer, never Treason to Nature's. Nature will

be closing her Picnic when you return to America,
but you will ride Home by sunset, which is far better.

I am glad you cherish the Sea. We correspond,
though I never met him.

I write in the midst of Sweet-Peas and by the side
of Orioles, and could put my hand on a Butterfly, only
he withdraws.

Touch Shakespeare for me.

"Be not afraid. The isle is full of noises, Sounds and sweet airs
that give delight and hurt not."

Fifty years now since World War II. She sits in the corner and
weeps.

And hurt not.

Six million dead.

"Well, we've been kept from ourselves long enough, don't you
think?"

We dare to speak. Trembling, and on the verge.

Extraordinary things have been written. Extraordinary things
will continue to be written.

Nineteen ninety-five: Vinyl makes its small comeback. To the
teenage music freak, to the classical music fiend, and to the
opera queen, CDs are now being disparaged as producing too
cold, too sanitary a sound. Vinyl is being sought out again for
its warmer, richer quality.

Wish: that we be open-minded and generous. That we fear not.

That the electronic page understand its powers and its limitations. Nothing replaces the giddiness one feels at the potential of hypertext. Entirely new shapes might be created, different ways of thinking, of perceiving.

Kevin Kelly, executive director of *Wired* magazine: "The first thing discovered by Jaron Lanier [the virtual reality pioneer] is to say what is reality? We get to ask the great questions of all time: what is life? What is human? What is civilization? And you ask it not in the way the old philosophers asked it, sitting in armchairs, but by actually trying it. Let's try and *make* life. Let's try and *make* community."

And now the Extropians, who say they can achieve immortality by downloading the contents of the human brain onto a hard disk. . . .

So turn to the students. Young visionaries. Who click on the Internet, the cyberworld in their sleep. Alvin Lu: citizen of the universe, the whole world at his fingertips. In love with the blinding light out there, the possibility, world without end, his love of all that is the future.

Let the fictions change shape, grow, accommodate. Let the medium change if it must; the artist persists.

You say all is doomed, but I say Julio Cortázar. I say Samuel Beckett. I say Marcel Proust. Virginia Woolf. I say García Lorca and Walt Whitman. I say Mallarmé. I say Ingeborg Bachmann. *The Apu Trilogy* will lie next to *Hamlet*. *Vivre Sa Vie* will live next to *Texts for Nothing*.

These fragmented prayers.

Making love around the fire of the alphabet.

Wish: that we not hurt each other purposely anymore.

A literature of love. A literature of tolerance. A literature of difference.

Saving the best of what was good in the old. Not to discard indiscriminately, but not to hold on too tightly, either. To go forward together, unthreatened for once.
The future is Robert Wilson and JLG. The future is Hou Hsiao-hsien. The future is Martha Graham, still.

The vocabularies of dance, of film, of performance.

The disintegration of categories.

If you say that language is dying, then what do you know of language?

I am getting a little tired of this you-and-I bit. But it tells me one important thing: *that I do not want it to have to be this way.* I do not believe it has to continue this way—you over there alternately blustery and cowering, me over here, defensive, angry.

Wish: a sky that is not divided. A way to look at the screen of the sky with its grandeur, its weather, its color, its patterns of bird flight, its airplanes and accidents and poisons, its mushroom clouds.

Its goldfinches frescoed against an aqua-blue dome.

Wish: that the sky go on forever. That we stop killing each other. That we allow each other to live.

April 1995 in New York City and the long-awaited Satyajit Ray Festival begins. For years he's been kept from us. Who decides, finally, what is seen, what is read, and why? And how much else has been deleted, omitted, neglected, ignored, buried, treated with utter indifference or contempt?

And in conversation with the man, my friend, a famous poet in fact, and the topic moved to someone we both knew who had just been operated on, and he said "masectomy," and I said back, "Yes, a mastectomy, a mastectomy," and he said "masectomy" like "vasectomy," and I said only under my breath, "It's mastectomy, idiot," ashamed, embarrassed, and a little intimidated, that was the worst part, a little unsure. That it made me question what I of course knew, that was the worst part— because of his easy confidence saying "masectomy," his arrogance, he hadn't even bothered to learn the right word, a *poet,* for God's sake, a man who worked with words, who should have known the right word for the removal of a breast, don't you think?

Mastectomy.

The undeniable danger of the sky.

Adrienne Rich: "Poetry means refusing the choice to kill or die."

Wish: that the straight white male give in just a little more gracefully. Call in its Michael Douglases, its suspect Hollywood, its hurt feelings, its fear—move over some.

After your thousands of years of affirmative action, give someone else a chance—just a chance.

The wish is for gentleness. The wish is for allowances.

"What is the phrase for the moon? And the phrase for love? By what name are we to call death? I do not know. I need a little language such as lovers use. . . ."

Wish: that the typical *New Yorker* story become the artifact it is and assume its proper place in the artifact museum, and not be mistaken for something still alive. Well we've just about had it with all the phony baloney, don't you think?

That the short story and the novel as they evolve and assume new, utterly original shapes might be treated gently. And with optimism. That is the wish.

That hypertext and all electronic writing still in its infancy be treated with something other than your fear and your contempt.

That, poised on the next century, we fear not. Make no grand pronouncements.

You say that language is dying, will die.

And at times I have felt for you, even loved you. But I have never believed you.

The Ebola virus is now. The Hanta virus. HIV. And that old standby, malaria. Live while you can. Tonight, who knows, may be our last. We may not even make the millennium, so don't worry about it so much.

All my friends who have died holding language in their throats, into the end. All my dead friends.

Cybernauts return from time to time wanting to see a smile instead of a colon followed by a closed parenthesis—the online sign for smile. When someone laughs out loud they want to hear real laughter in the real air, not just the letters LOL in front of them. Ah, yes. World while there is world.

A real bird in the real sky and then perhaps a little prose poem or something in the real sky, or the page or the screen or the human heart, pulsing.

> I do not know which to prefer,
> The beauty of inflections
> Or the beauty of innuendoes,
> The blackbird whistling
> Or just after.

One world.

The future of literature is utopic. As surely as my friends Ed and Alan will come this weekend to visit, bearing rose lentils. As long as one can say "rose," can say "lentil."

Gary dying, saying "Kappa maki."

You say, *over.* But I say, *no.*

I say faith and hope and trust and forever right next to wretched and hate and misery and hopeless.

In the future we will finally be allowed to live, just as we are, to imagine, to glow, to pulse.

Let the genres blur if they will. Let the genres redefine themselves.

Language is a woman, a rose constantly in the process of opening.

Vibrant, irresistible, incandescent.

Whosoever has allowed the villanelle to enter them or the sonnet. Whosoever has let in one genuine sentence, one paragraph, has felt that seduction like a golden thread being pulled slowly through one....

Wish: that forms other than those you've invented or sanctioned through your thousands of years of privilege might arise and be celebrated.

"Put another way, it seems to me that we have to rediscover everything about everything. There is only one solution, and that is to turn one's back on American cinema....Up until now we have lived in a closed world. Cinema fed on cinema, imitating itself. I now see that in my first films I did things because I had already seen them in the cinema. If I showed a police inspector drawing a revolver from his pocket, it wasn't because the logic of the situation I wanted to describe demanded it, but because I had seen police inspectors in other films drawing revolvers at this precise moment and in this precise way. The same thing has happened in painting. There have been periods of organization and imitation and periods of rupture. We are now in a period of rupture. We must turn to life again. We must move into modern life with a virgin eye."
—*Jean-Luc Godard, 1966*

Wish: that Alvin Lu might wander in the astounding classroom of the world through time and space, endlessly inspired, endlessly enthralled by what he finds there. That he be allowed to reinvent freely, revel freely.

My professor once and now great friend, Barbara Page, out there too, ravenous, furious, and without fear, inventing whole new worlds, ways of experiencing the text. New freedoms.

The world doesn't end, says Charles Simic. Engraved on our foreheads in ash, turned into a language of stars or birdsong across a vast sky; it stays. Literature doesn't end—but it may change shapes, be capable of things we cannot even imagine yet.

Woolf: "What is the phrase for the moon? And the phrase for love? By what name are we to call death? I do not know. I need a little language such as lovers use, words of one syllable such as children speak when they come into the room and find their mother sewing and pick up the scrap of bright wool, a feather, or a shred of chintz. I need a howl; a cry."

Charlotte Brontë: "My sister Emily loved the moors. Flowers brighter than the rose bloomed in the blackest of the heath for her; out of a sullen hollow in the livid hillside her mind could make an Eden. She found in the bleak solitude many and dear delights; and not the least and best loved was—liberty."

The future will be gorgeous and reckless, and words, those luminous charms, will set us free again. If only for a moment.

Whosoever has allowed the language of lovers to enter them, the language of wound and pain and solitude and hope. Whosoever has dug in the miracle of the earth. Mesmerizing dirt, earth, word.

Allowed love in. Allowed despair in.

Words are the ginger candies my dying friends have sucked on. Or the salve of water.

Precious words, contoured by silence. Informed by the pressure of the end.

Words are the crow's feet embedded in the skin of the father I love. Words are like that to me, still.

Words are the music of her hair on the pillow.

Words are the lines vibrating in the forest or in the painting. Pressures that enter us—bisect us, order us, disorder us, unite us, free us, help us, hurt us, cause anxiety, pleasure, pain.

Words are the footprints as they turn away in the snow.

There is no substitute for the language I love.

My father, one state away but still too far, asks over the telephone if I might take a photo of this bluebird, the first I have ever seen, because he hears how filled with delight I am by this fleeting sighting. But it's so tiny, it flies so fast, it's so hard to see. So far away. Me, with my small hunk of technology, pointing. With my nostalgia machine. My box that says fleeting, my box that says future.

My pleasure machine. My weeping machine that dreams: keep.

This novel that says desire and fleeting and unfinished.

Unfinished and left that way. Unfinished, not abandoned. Unfinished, not because of death or indifference or loss of faith, or nerve, just unfinished.

Not to draw false conclusions anymore. Not to set up false polarities. Unfinished and left that way, if necessary.

To allow everyone to write, to thrive, to live.

The Baltimore oriole returned from its American tropics at the edge of this frame now. I wait.

On this delicious precipice.

And nothing replaces this hand moving across the page, as it does now, intent on making a small mark and allowing it to stand on this longing surface.

Writing *oriole*. Imagining freedom. All that is possible.

April in the country. My hands in the dark earth, or the body of a woman, or any ordinary, gorgeous sentence.

Whosoever has let the hand linger on a burning thigh, or a shining river of light....

Whosoever has allowed herself to be dazzled by the motion of the alphabet,

or has let music into the body. Or has allowed music to fall onto the page.

Wish: to live and allow others to live. To sing and allow others to sing—while we can.

And hurt not.

Fleeting and longing moment on this earth. We were lucky to be here.

I close my eyes and hear the intricate chamber music of the world. An intimate, complicated, beautiful conversation in every language, in every tense, in every possible medium and form—incandescent.

—for Alvin, Barbara, and Judith
1 June 1995

Like the clarinet with the flute, like the French horn with the oboe, like the violin and the piano—take the melody from me, when it's time.

25 April 1995
Germantown, New York

A walk around the loop and I notice the bloodroot has begun to bloom. A bluebird, two bluebirds! The first I've ever seen, over by the convent. Before my eyes I see an infant clasping a small bird as depicted in Renaissance painting and sculpture. The world begins again. In this vision. In the words *bloodroot* and *bluebird.* And the goldfinches too are suddenly back. Today I saw three enormous turtles sunning themselves at a pond. The bliss of being on leave from teaching is beyond description. I recall Dickinson when someone mused that time must go very slowly for her, saying, "Time! Why time was all I wanted!" And so ditto. Blissful time. Writing, walking every day. I am keeping depression at bay, mania in check. All private sufferings and hurt are somehow more manageable here in solitude. The moment seems all now. The imaginative event, the natural event (two wild turkeys in the woods), the sexual event, and the constantly changing and evolving forms in language for all of this. John sends a note to remind me that my essay is due for the *Review of Contemporary Fiction* on May 1, but that I may have a small extension. I should be finishing up *Defiance,* but all I can think about are my erotic études— again feeling on the threshold of something amazing and out of reach. I'm extremely excited—hard to describe—my brain feels unhinged…

I must make a note as to where to move the daffodils, the iris. The earth in my hands. A wand of forsythia like a light in my hands. I think of Barbara an hour away, the glowing glyphs coming off the screen in her study. The whole world— luminous, luminous. We were lucky to be here. Even in pain and uncertainty and rage and fear—some fear. In exhaustion.

Too much energy has gone into this Brown/Columbia deci- sion. Where shall I end up? I have only partially succeeded in keeping it all in its proper place. I've had to work too hard to keep my mind at the proper distance. It takes its toll. I've needed the space to think, to dream other things. It hardly matters today though; another étude brews.

The *RCF* essay now in the back of my head. What to say? What can be said? How to use it to learn something, explore something I need to explore. When thinking of literature, the past and the present all too often infuriate me: everyone, everything that's been kept out. The future won't, can't be the same and yet…one worries about it. What I wonder most is if there is a way, whether there might be a way in this whole wide world, to forgive them. Something for the sake of my own work, my own life I need to do—have needed to do a long time. Perhaps in my essay I will make an attempt, the first movement toward some sort of reconciliation, at any rate. If it's possible. To set up the drama that might make it possible.

This breakable heart.

April. How poised everything seems. How wonderfully ready. And I, too, trembling—and on the verge…